Lily

Your dreams are closer
than you think!

Lily

Christina Gunn

Roseway Publishing Co. Ltd.
Lockeport, Nova Scotia

Roseway Publishing gratefully acknowledges the support of the Canada Council and the Nova Scotia Department of Education, Cultural Affairs Division.

Illustrations: Raymond Price
Cover and book design: Brenda Conroy
Proofreader: Michèle Raymond
Printed and bound in Canada by
Hignell Printing, Winnipeg, Manitoba

Published by Roseway Publishing Co. Ltd.
Lockeport, Nova Scotia B0T 1L0
phone/fax (902) 656-2223
email ktudor@atcon.com

Canadian Cataloguing in Publication Data
Gunn, Christina.

Lily
ISBN 1-896496-06-7

I. Title.
PS8563.U5717L5 1998 jC813'.54 C98-950202-3
PZ7.G86Li 1998

To all my friends and family at
L'Arche Cape Breton
and elsewhere.

The Beginning

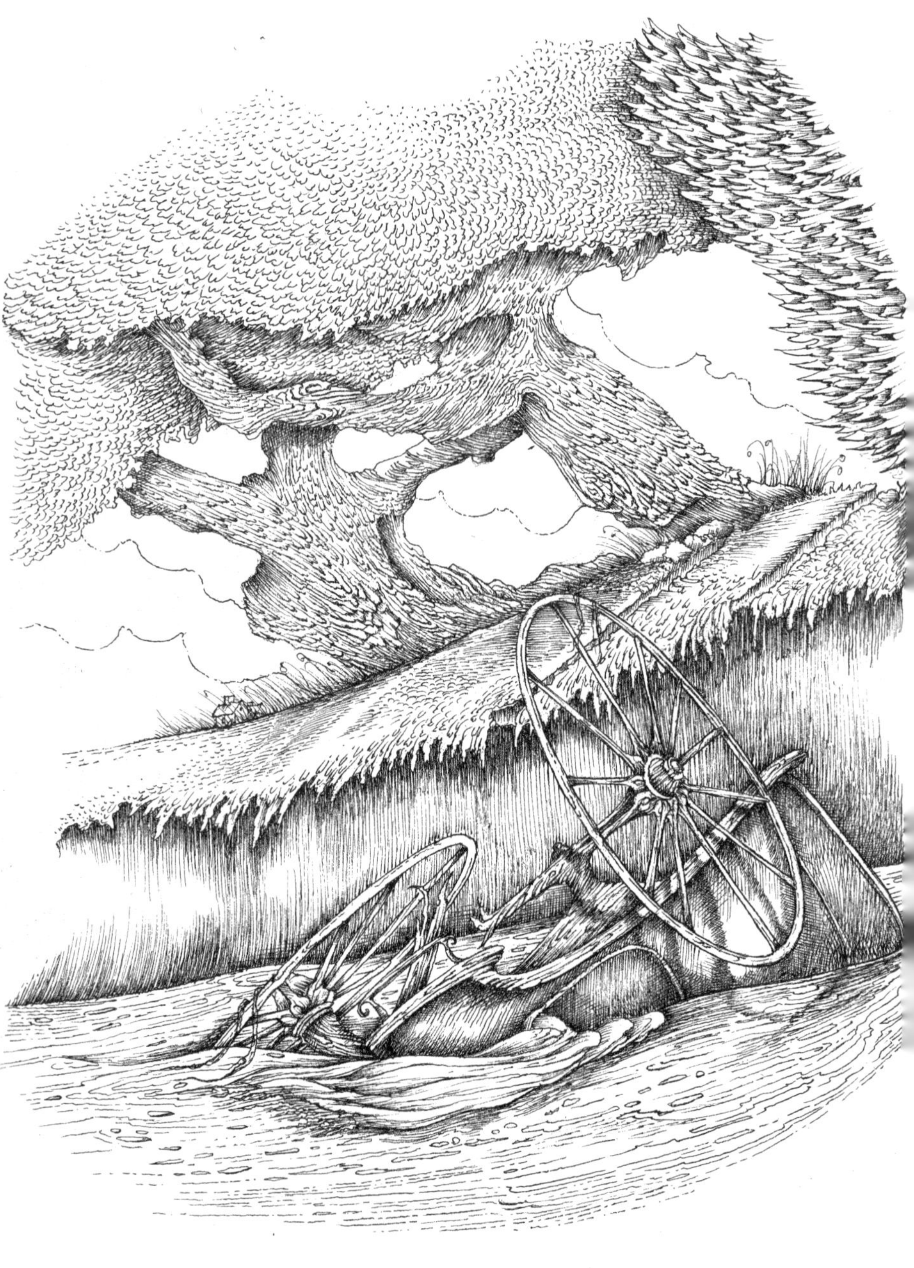

Two Graves

"I'm cold," Marian whispered, tugging at her nurse's cloak. "It's raining again."

"Really, child!" the large woman growled, tilting her head and talking through clenched teeth. "You've lived here all your life. I'd have thought you'd be used to the rain by now! Besides, you wanted to come here."

No. Now that was not true. Marian frowned. She had wanted to see Lily. Instead, she was standing inside the huge iron gates of the graveyard, staring obediently at the two coffins, one large and one small.

The adults thought she didn't know Lily was gone, as though she couldn't see the pain in Robin's eyes when he scurried past her. The adults spoke about the "accident," as they called it, in hushed voices. Whenever they thought she was listening, they broke off and returned to their discussions of husbands and dresses and how long they had been working on that particular bit of needlework.

The children were less shy. It had become a delightful new game to get Marian to cry by describing the deaths very vividly. None knew exactly what had happened to the Fitzooths, but most held two very strong beliefs: that Lily had drowned and that Lily's brother Robin was going crazy. Marian never told them how Robin sat in Lily's room now, gazing out the open window for hours on end. Sometimes, he slept there. Those children had never understood Robin and Lily. They wouldn't understand his grief either.

She glanced across the coffins at him now. How lonely he looked without his usual flamboyant companion! He seemed deaf to all the sniffling going on around him, staring at the coffins with a kind of solemn horror in his eyes.

"Ashes to ashes . . ." the priest intoned, ". . . dust to dust . . ."

"Let's go." Marian tugged at her nurse's arm.

"Wait, child. We'll go soon." She shook off the nine-year-old impatiently.

"I want to go now!" The priest's voice was still droning on in the background, and the ropes began to creak as the coffins were lowered. Marian turned, and walked away, shutting out the sound. She could hear the nurse racing up behind her, scolding already.

"That was a bad-mannered thing to do, child, and at a funeral! What do you suppose young master

Robin thought of that?"

"I don't believe he even saw I was there. What does it matter that I left?"

"Really, child!" The nurse drew in a gasp through her teeth, then shook her head, already oblivious to the little girl beside her. "Peculiar family, though. I always knew that little maid would get herself in trouble. If there had been just a bit more discipline! Discipline is the key to everything! Really! To let a child run wild like that! Thought they could dress her up for mass and that would be enough, but it didn't fool me! Letting those two children play together all day! And your parents agreeing to your doing the same! Why . . ."

"My parents can do as they like!" Marian snapped at the older woman. "My father liked Lily. He gave her a locket for her birthday and told her to never grow up, and now she won't! So watch what you say, or I'll tell my father and he'll hire a new governess for me!"

Marian stormed away, the older woman following her, nervously twisting her skirt in her hands. "Discipline. That's what these children need," she muttered under her breath as the graveyard faded behind them.

Robin

Robin curled up into a ball in the corner of Lily's room, glaring at the luxurious furnishings of it as though wanting to blame them for his sister's death. He'd wrapped a cloak of his mother's around him, breathing in the still lingering scent of lilac that had clung to her.

"Lily," he whispered at the walls, but they were only stone and did not answer him. Robin longed for his mother's voice and arms to comfort him, or his sister's quick smile and dark eyes to draw him out of his grief, but they were dead and he could only cry, the sobs shaking his young body, tears coursing down his face. The tears only served to remind him of the fatal trip.

It leapt to his mind in snatches. He could see the horses slipping on the mud as they sprang back from whatever had startled them, and the carriage tipping, and then water. Everywhere was water. And he could see Lily, could see her fighting to stay afloat, but being pulled down by the dress that Mother had forced her to wear, the petticoats sopping up water with every second that she remained there. And the rocks and the current, and she disappeared. And then there was only the white shrouded figure of Mother, and the empty memorial to Lily.

"Robin?"

He didn't turn around, but furiously wiped the tears from his eyes. Hugh Fitzooth watched his son with pain and he laid a hand on Robin's head.

"Robin . . ." The words didn't come and when he looked at Lily's deserted room he could hear her laughter and his own grief enveloped him.

"It was a fine funeral." It was all he could manage to say.

Robin did not move. "She wasn't even there. How can you have a funeral without a body?"

"We looked for her."

"If you had looked you would have found her!"

"Let it go, Robin! She is dead. They both are dead! The sooner we accept that the better!" His voice fell again. "It's just us now."

Robin had not moved throughout the outburst. He still sat staring at the wall. Only his lips moved.

"Lily is not dead."

"Don't pretend anymore, Robin! She is gone!"

"She's not dead!" Robin spoke just above a whisper. "I'd know it if she was."

Lily Awakens

She was cold and wet and she hurt all over. The rough stone she lay against bit at her cheek and hands, while a mixture of cool water and her own blood lapped against her lips. It tasted bitter in her mouth, but she made no effort to spit it out, only lay there looking with wide eyes at her surroundings.

The forest rose dark and mysterious and wild on either side of the river in which she lay. The river was wild too. It pushed past the girl, deep to one side of the rock she leaned against, and shallow on the other. The deeper water gushed between rocks and boulders, smashing into whatever it met.

The trees rose high from the forest floor, glistening with rain, giants reaching to the skies, never touching it, but close. The wide spaces beneath the trees were gloomy, despite their openness. The air smelled vaguely of sap and wet earth. From somewhere close by rose the strong smell of wet dog.

It was now that the puppy chose to place a large clumsy paw on her eyes. She sat up abruptly and he toppled off her back, into the river. With a fierce wagging of his tail, he scrambled onto shore, seeming very relieved to find her alive. His little pink tongue lolled from his mouth, hanging sideways in a smile.

She staggered to her feet, but a wave of nausea overtook her and she fell back into the water, her head pounding. She lay back, letting the water cascade over her head, erasing some of the pain. It washed blood and mud into her mouth and she sat up again. Focusing on the tan body of the Great Dane puppy on the shore, she pulled herself to her knees, and crawled slowly and painfully across the rough stones. Her knees were raw and scraped by the time she reached the shore, the heels of her hands rubbed red. She sat with her knees under her chin and shivered, her shredded dress letting the damp wind blow against her skin.

When she looked up again, a dark colt was leaning over her, wet and muddy, his long mane and tail matted with leaves. He nuzzled her with his velvet muzzle and snorted softly in her ear, his whiskers brushing the sensitive skin there. It seemed perfectly natural that he should be there, perfectly normal. The girl laughed and finally released the grip on her knees. Her hands went limp as she relaxed them and she turned her face away from the horse, trying to hide from his tickling caresses.

She saw her hands. Something there, some entire sense of unbeing, had never let her stop and wonder, but now this hand, these fingers . . . they were hers. They bent at her will, opened and closed, wrinkling the skin that was hers. And that hand belonged to this body, named . . . and the thoughts stopped.

She frowned and turned to the puppy, digging at his collar, her eager fingers tracing the letters burnt into his collar.

"Giant," she said softly. "You're Giant."

Now the fingers turned on herself, tugging at clothing and digging into pockets. Something cool and smooth leapt to their touch. She pulled it out carefully, the chain first and then the locket with a name engraved on its silver surface.

"Lily. That must be me."

The name sounded alien to her. She turned it over on her tongue once more. Lily. It was a good name, she was sure. More importantly, it was hers. And the locket was hers. She tightened her fingers around the piece of jewelry as though she'd never let go.

Lily stood up, staggered, then stood straight again. Slowly, carefully, she stepped up to the young horse, took hold of its halter and rubbed the velvet nose.

"You're beautiful," she whispered as her fingers darted over its halter and body, looking for a name or brand. His rich black coat shone in the sunlight, broken only by a white star and the streak that ran back from it, disappearing among the black hair of the mane.

"You have no name, though," Lily said, still searching for a sign of one as the horse began to nibble on the hair that grew at the nape of her neck. "If you were mine, I would call you Starline." She smiled, scrunching up her shoulders as its whiskers tickled her skin. "I guess you are mine now."

With one hand under the halter, she walked ahead, not knowing where she was going or why. She just needed to find . . . something, although even she did not know what it was.

As they walked, Lily's head grew heavier and her feet dragged and the world seemed to be moving extraordinarily slowly and everything echoed in her head. She leaned against Starline, breathing in the warm smell of living, moving horseflesh, until the world finally reeled around and she sank to the ground, exhausted, her head pounding outwards as though it would explode. Every bone in her body ached and every muscle. The singing birds sounded like a harsh blare of trumpets, the movement of her clothes like crashing waves and the scraping of Giant's claws made her want to bury her head in the cold earth, away from all sound.

Opening her eyes, Lily crawled wearily over to Giant, pulling him away from his digging by the scruff of his neck, and curled up beside him.

She was looking directly into the hole Giant had dug, but it wasn't a hole. It was a mess of torn vines. From under the greenery glinted metal. Still lying on her side, Lily reached her hand up to the metal, pulling the vines slowly away from the wood that they covered, away from the door that they hid.

She didn't move right away, just lay there, running her fingers up and down the wood. Then, with a great deal of effort, she pulled herself up onto her feet. She leaned against the carved wooden door, then pushed it open and stepped inside.

A long hall stretched in front of her, carved completely out of the stone of the hill, broken only by an orderly row of doors on either side. Each door was like the one she had just stepped through: heavy wood, carved and without locks. A wooden cross was carved into each one, a reminder of the monks who had inhabited it once.

There was no sign of another person in the dim outlines the darkness revealed to her. Rat droppings lay scattered over the floor and cobwebs hung from the ceiling in any place not already occupied by a furry carpet of sleeping bats.

She moved slowly over the dirt, and unseen creatures scurried from her path.

At the end of the hallway was another door and beside it was a small opening, almost hidden in the shadows. Inside this niche was a narrow flight of stone steps curving upward. With a hand pressed against either wall, she began to climb.

The second floor was a model of the first one, only the ceiling was lower and rounder and the entire hallway was shorter in length. It was a little cleaner. Perhaps the rats didn't climb stairs very well.

She entered the third room to her right. It was a small square one with one, lone, moss-covered window beside a bed. Lily moved slowly across the room to the window and began pulling the covering away in dark, damp handfuls.

Sunlight now reached into the room, touching first on the short bed and its tattered bedcovers, just below the window. Still in the shadows, a rough brown tunic lay neatly folded on a small, dusty chair with one of its fat legs broken. Lily pressed down the chair and it teetered ominously, so she left only her handprint there, a child's handprint, laced with blood.

She stepped back into the hallway, eyeing the five doors across from her and the two on either side, but not approaching them. She turned back to the stairs and, on reaching the ground outside, breathed in the fresh air gratefully.

A wide glade stretched out before her. To her left was what remained of a garden, but was now only a cemetery of sticks and string holding up a harvest of weeds. To her right was a pasture with silky golden grass and fallen fence posts, pulled down by winding plants. Throughout the clearing ran a path, weathered by too many feet to easily give up to the forest. It twisted and turned, darting away with promises of delightful destinations, and eventually leading Lily down to a spring. There was a deep pool in the center of the spring, deep enough to swim in, filled with a dark water. At its edge, where Lily stood, it was just deep enough for wading.

Lily cautiously stripped off her bloodied dress, letting it drop beside her in a tattered heap of lavender silk. Lowering her bruised body into the water, she clung to the shore. The sun shone lazily on the naked figure sitting in water up to her waist, clutching her legs to herself. She was home.

Hunger

The coach bounced unpleasantly over a rock, jostling its two dignified passengers. As the vehicle continued to rattle them, the woman frowned.

"Is that really necessary?" she complained, leaning back against the lush cushions piled around her and clutching a rather large kitten to her.

"What, dear?" her husband Henry asked, rubbing his dark grey beard.

"The speed. It's frightfully upsetting," she pouted, stroking the cat with a slim hand that glittered with rings.

"Oh. I'll see to it." Henry stuck his head out the window, calling loudly to the driver. "I say, is all this speed necessary? We're in no hurry."

The driver didn't slow down or even turn his head. "Look behind you, Milord."

He did. Not far behind them came an enormous black horse, carrying a small rider who crouched low in the saddle, urging the animal ahead. There were no obvious markings on the worn tack or tattered clothes of the rider and Henry frowned in puzzlement.

"Who would be riding here?"

"Bandits." The driver warned. "Better get inside, Milord."

Henry withdrew his head then and settled himself on the cushions with a frown wrinkling his brow.

"Well, Henry?"

"What? Oh. It does seem necessary, Agatha."

"Whatever do you mean? Good heavens!" She had turned to the window while speaking and, while she did so, the black horse came alongside their coach. Its rider was a child of about ten years of age, wearing boy's clothes that were much too big for her and a dagger at her waist.

"A dagger!" Henry yelled. "She's armed!"

"I know, Milord," the driver shouted back.

His wife clutched Henry's arm. "That man has to go, Henry! We are in danger here and he doesn't do anything! Why . . . !"

The girl had her right foot in the left stirrup and balanced for a moment before flinging herself onto the coach, gripping onto the window fiercely. Instantly, the dagger appeared, glinting. The coach weaved suddenly, but she managed to keep her grip, moving with the motion of the vehicle.

"Don't move." Her voice was that of an adult and Henry watched her face with a peculiar fascination. He had never seen such hunger before and it enthralled him. She had none of that childish roundness he knew from his own children; only gaunt cheeks and large, intense brown eyes.

"Don't stare at me!" He dropped his eyes, watching instead the dagger in her hand. "Pass me that basket, over there."

"It's only our dinner. There's nothing valuable in there!" The girl ignored the woman speaking to her, watching only the basket.

"Is there much?"

"Yes."

"For one lunch?" She glanced at Henry's rather large belly and nodded. "I guess so." The basket was emptied into a large sack she produced from inside her baggy clothes and the girl began to withdraw from the window. Suddenly, she paused.

"What is that?" Her eyes watched the oversized kitten as it gnawed on the fine gold chain attaching it to its owner's wrist.

"Only Fluffy. She's a good little baby, isn't she?" The woman crooned to the cat, who hissed loudly.

"I want her."

"What?!"

"I want her." Her voice was determined and her eyes piercing.

"I don't . . . Henry!" The woman was whining now, her hands tightening on the wriggling animal. "You can't expect me to . . ."

"I think you'd better."

Agatha pouted, unlacing the chain from her wrist.

"She's not an ordinary cat, little girl," she sulked, handing the spitting creature over. The girl put it in a pouch at her waist and smiled threateningly, leaning back towards the black horse that still ran alongside the coach.

"And I'm not a little girl." Suddenly, she was gone. The extra set of hoofbeats slowed, then stopped and when Henry poked his head out the window, he could see the girl by the roadside, gobbling down his lunch with all the ferocity of a forest beast and with an uncertain, wild beauty.

Peter

Peter

In the darkness Peter opened his eyes. Sounds echoed in the night outside of the small cottage and the bit of deer meat he had eaten caused uneasiness in his stomach. It was not hunger. Hunger he was used to. It was gnawing fear.

His wife, Molly, stirred beside him. "Peter?" she whispered. "What's wrong?" Her voice was sleepy and he only shrugged in answer.

"Go back to sleep."

"Don't worry," she sighed, rolling over and closing her eyes. "You buried the carcass deep."

Her breath slowed and became the peaceful rhythm of sleep. Peter carefully stepped over the trundle bed on which little Anna slept and made his way across the room. Moonlight flickered through the doorway, guiding him through the cramped quarters. Slowly he made his way to the door and outside.

The pasture lay before him. The empty fields and barn were quiet and still. The land had never been his, but he still looked upon it with pride.

Of course, the land was too rich for him. All land was too rich for him.

He turned his eyes to where he had buried his kill, far from the house, and he stopped. Three figures bent low to the ground above where the deer lay. Peter's breath stopped in his throat. The three figures were digging.

Hastily, he turned away and stumbled about in the darkness until he found his clothes piled neatly beside the bed. Molly moved and he froze, but she did not wake. He continued to dress.

He stepped out the door, closing it softly behind him. He didn't look back at the diggers, but moved in the opposite direction, toward the forest. Behind him he heard a triumphant shout as the diggers found the deer and then footsteps, running towards the house. Peter did not slow down.

"Oh, God," he prayed. "Protect them!"

The forest closed around him and he cursed it all, the darkness, the forest and the poverty that had forced him here. Water fell against his face and he sighed. Rain. Of course. And so he cursed the rain, simply because it was there.

The rain blinded him, mixing with tears and anger, until the forest had swallowed him completely and he whirled around in despair, lost. The trees rose above him, letting him catch glimpses of the sky, but no more. The sky seemed bright against the darkness of the trees. An owl called in the distance and the night whispers echoed in his ears. He leaned back against the hill behind him . . . and fell. The solid mass gave way and he toppled forward onto a damp stone floor.

It was silent here, in this dark cave, and warm. He closed the door that had given way against his weight, frowning, puzzled, at it. Then he turned away, letting his senses lead him in the dim light. A fire crackled nearby, sending flickering light out into a tight circle around itself. The scent of roasting venison wafted toward him, and now he didn't care who was there, watching in the darkness. The deer he had killed had been so small that it had barely filled Molly and Anna's stomachs, much less his own. Peter's practically empty stomach erupted into a churning frenzy and he plunged ahead.

The sword shone as the cold blade stabbed at his chest, leaping out of the darkness to stop him. Its owner crouched in semi-darkness, the light falling on her dark eyes. The coolness of them was terrifying.

"Don't move." Her voice was low and threatening.

"I wasn't planning to."

"Very wise of you." She eyed him furiously. "Who are you?"

"Peter Semmons. A farmer."

"Where do you come from?"

"Guy of Gisbourne's land."

She growled softly. "Why are you here?"

"It was an accident . . ."

"Answer the question."

"I leaned against the door and fell in." He eyed her. She was young, about fourteen, with huge angry eyes. "Is there anyone else here?"

"I'm asking the questions." She bit her lip. "Why are you out here? No one comes out this far." She laughed. "The goblins might get you."

"I was afraid."

"Of goblins?" Her voice was cold and sarcastic, tired of superstitious villagers.

"No. Of Foresters."

Her face grew deadly serious once again at the mention of the ruthless rangers that stalked the woods of Nottingham. "And you came here?" He nodded and she let out a strangled curse. "Were you followed?"

"No."

"Are you sure?"

"Believe me."

"Why should I?" she cried, her words echoing in the darkness and Peter was sure he saw the shadows move. Something snarled behind him.

"What was that?" he whispered, so as not to startle whatever it was. She ignored his question.

"Why were they chasing you?"

"I killed . . . poached a deer." She said nothing. "They took it." He shrugged, waiting for her to break the silence. It was then that the two creatures stepped into the light.

Their lips and fangs were stained with fresh blood and they stretched their tawny bodies before the fire. The cat kneaded her talons, rubbing her back against the dog. Each move was casually menacing. Both watched Peter warily.

The girl glanced first at the cat, then at the dog, and back at Peter. "Are you hungry?" The question was so unexpected that he jumped and the blade came unpleasantly close to his skin. "Well?"

He shrugged, unsure of how to react, then nodded furiously. She took the blade away, walked past the animals, lifted the spit and laid the entire cut of meat in front of him.

"Eat." Peter looked at her face again. Her eyes weren't actually as huge as he had thought. It was only that her face was thin, although not as thin as most he knew. He glanced at the meat, then back at her. How long since she'd eaten?

"I . . . I couldn't."

Her eyes flashed.

"Eat it!" The enticing smell bit at him and he needed little more persuasion. They both sat on the floor. He ate, while she watched silently. The meat against his tongue had an unusually smoky taste from the fire. It was the first time he could remember that his stomach felt at all full. Even the deer he had poached had been split three ways, and it had been a small beast.

As soon as the last mouthful was swallowed, she spoke.

"Poacher?"

He nodded.

"You realize the family, yours in this case, will likely have to pay a fine?"

"How much?" He licked his fingers nervously, thinking of the empty money pouch at home and of the numerous debts he'd unwillingly compiled.

"Anywhere from five to fifteen gold pieces."

"Fifteen!" He stared at her, realizing how impossible even the five would be. He had seen the women taken away by the soldiers and had heard rumours of their lives in the palace. He thought of Molly, still so young, and he was afraid.

"I can get it for you."

"How?"

She shrugged. "Many people have more than they need. They don't even notice if some goes astray."

"Steal it?"

She nodded.

"For me?"

"I don't do favours." He frowned, uncomprehending, and she met his gaze coolly.

"Frankly, I'm good at it, but there is a certain amount of risk . . ."

"What do you want from me?"

"Live here."

"Pardon?"

She shrugged again. "I need a farmer. Can't live on what I hunt and can't easily buy what I need. I do have a price on my head, you know." She grinned proudly, obviously pleased with the fact.

"I don't want help from a . . ."

"Thief?" Her smile faded.

"I don't want stolen money!"

"Shut up!" she snarled. "This isn't the world you think it is."

"But . . ."

"You're an outlaw too, you know." She almost spit the words at him and they stung bitterly. "Now, do I help you or not?"

"I'll only dig myself deeper."

She shrugged. "They don't care. The punishment is always the same. If you leave here now, they'll catch you before you go three steps."

"And you can help me?" He instantly felt sorry for the sarcasm that fell so easily from his tongue. She turned away.

"How do you think I survived? I know how! You don't know this life, or how to live it!"

"I suppose that is true . . ."

"Then stay." She held out her hand. Peter took

it slowly and she smiled, a real smile, free of sarcasm. “Good choice, Mister Semmons. Maybe you will make it after all.”

She stood up and disappeared into the darkness. “Find a room. Sleep in it. There are plenty to choose from. Tomorrow, you’ll get the money.”

“Wait! What’s your name?”

It floated back to him, through the silence, wrapping itself around the flickering flames.

“Lily.”

The Ties That Bind

He awoke cold, wrapped in a tight cocoon of threadbare blankets. The room was still dark, ivy closing over the window, swallowing light. He lay still, wishing for Molly and for Anna, for all the morning noises that they made together, the delicate game of waking him up, although they knew that he was already awake. He missed the way Anna would climb on his chest, trying to pry open his eyelids and then shrieking as he leapt up out of his "sleep" and grabbed her, tumbling out of the bed together. Meanwhile, Molly would stand at the table, adopting a frown and saying that if they didn't sit down right now she'd have to eat all the food herself and then what would they do? But there very rarely was any food. He cried, a deep, forlorn sobbing that echoed in his ears.

When he looked up, Lily stood against the door, her face confused and sad, her fingers laced around the locket at her throat. Peter swallowed the rest of his tears and wiped his eyes hurriedly, angry at the intrusion. Lily said nothing.

"Well," he finally snapped at her. "Let's get on with it!"

Lily shrugged and turned away. This time she didn't grow angry at his rough words. Her boyish figure slouched as she walked away and he regretted the harshness of his voice.

She picked up a short sword at the outer doorway and paused, looking back at him over her shoulder. "Are you coming?" she said softly. Without waiting for an answer, she left.

Peter sighed and followed her, stumbling out of his door and then outside, into the forest. She didn't pause, walking silently and leading a large stallion. Peter jogged to catch up with her, then casually walked beside the stallion, not looking at the girl. She did not turn her head.

They reached the road in silence. Peter quickly slumped against the nearest tree, watching Lily mount and silently cursing himself. In the distance he could hear wheels clattering and the trotting of a horse. Lily tensed in the saddle.

A peasant cart went by and she relaxed, ignoring the pitiful cart with its pile of rescued rubbish and the sway-backed nag that pulled it. Lily's horse did not even glance at the vehicle, only took the opportunity to steal some grass.

"Don't do that," Lily scolded. Peter glanced at her guiltily, then relaxed as the stallion obediently lifted its head.

But then Lily leaned forward in the saddle, her face suddenly eager. Soon the sound of hoof-beats reached Peter's ears, the high-stepping trot of well-bred animals. He tensed as Lily balanced her knife in one hand and crouched low in the saddle.

The coach burst into view, running hard, and passed them. Lily's horse exploded from the forest, Lily balanced in the stirrups. She then put both feet in one stirrup, gripping the horse's mane. Peter watched in suspense, his heart racing, fascinated.

She leapt onto the moving coach and scampered up into the driver's seat, roughly pushing the driver away. The coach slowed, stopped, and began to back up.

It stopped in front of Peter. Lily was holding the reins, a wicked smile on her face. "Okay. Let's see what we need."

Avoiding looking at the frightened occupants, Peter approached the coach and glanced around the compartment.

"There's nothing here I can use." He looked at Lily. "We should have stopped the other. It had farming tools."

"Don't tell me how or what to steal! I doubt that farmer would have been very happy to donate!"

"These people aren't either."

Lily shrugged. "They have more to spare."

"But not what we need."

Sighing, she jumped down and shoved past the couple inside. Her light fingers danced over purses and jewelry before she turned to Peter again.

"This is all you need." She poured the money into his hands. "Buy what you need."

Peter stared at the pile of gold in his hand, more than he had ever seen. "Why don't you buy your own tools?"

She laughed, leaning against the coach and counting out gold pieces from one of the purses. "You must be joking. There are too many people in town! Me, go shopping?"

"Well, if I'm an outlaw too, how can I go?"

Lily shrugged. "You have friends, don't you? Somehow I doubt that your villagers would turn you in."

Peter didn't look up. His hands holding the jewels trembled, then began to shake violently. "This is wrong," he whispered hoarsely.

Lily looked up."Wrong? Of course it's wrong! It's also wrong for them to have so much and for you and your family to starve! I don't care if it's wrong! This is life! Get used to it!"

She grabbed the gold from him and thrust it into her pouch angrily. Then she stormed to the coach, throwing the reins at the driver. "Get out of here!" she screamed, her voice harsh. "Run far, far away from me!"

The horses bolted away and Lily watched them go, her face relaxing slowly. She turned and threw the money bag at Peter.

"Here," she said softly. "I've kept my part of the deal."

She disappeared into the forest. Peter stared at the money in his hands. Now, he belonged to her.

The First Gift

Peter sat back in the dirt, balancing on the balls of his feet and wiping the sweat from his eyes. He glanced at the long rows of freshly plowed earth, the crooked rows that had taken too long to plow, for neither the horse nor Lily knew what to do and neither was any help.

Oh, Lily tried, but she knew absolutely nothing and only grew impatient, retreating into the woods until she returned with bags of gold or food. He did not ask where it came from. He ate it and was happy, as she was, for as farming was his release, thievery was hers.

"Peter?" He jumped. Lily had come on a thief's feet and spoken into his ear, a quiet voice that startled him. He turned around. She stood looking at her feet, at the rolled up legs of the too-big pants. A bag was clutched in her arms. She shoved it at him.

"Here."

He looked inside, unsure, and pulled out the doll. It was plain, with a simple peasant's costume and coarse horsehair, but it was something few children could afford to own. Lily did not meet his gaze, only smiled, embarrassed.

"It's for Anna." She smiled again."I thought that maybe you might want to go home today."

He looked at the doll. "Whose was it?"

"I bought it from a woman passing by." She smiled. "She makes them. I thought it nicer than one of the richer china dolls."

He nodded. "And I may go home?"

"Oh, you can go home whenever you wish, to visit, but you must come back before the soldiers realize that you have gone home." The embarrassed look began to fade. "The outside will kill you if you stay too long."

She turned away, then paused, lingering. "Do you miss them? Your family?"

"Yes."

"It must be nice." She ducked her head and darted away.

Molly's Charity

Molly nervously clenched and unclenched her fingers against the fabric of her skirt as she walked, muttering over and over the speech she had rehearsed. She had had Lily over to her house many times, but had never gone to her, had never had to ask her for anything. Now she moved through the forest, trying to follow directions which she had only half listened to, for what need had she to come to the cave? What need indeed!

Finally she came to the hill, a rather obvious mound of vines and moss-covered stone, but she knew that she would have ignored it if she hadn't been looking for it. For who would imagine such a dwelling so deep within the forest? She pulled away the carefully placed vines, revealing a door, and she finally entered her husband's new home.

It was bigger than she had thought it would be, more civilized. It was not as clean as her own home, but was not the filth that she had expected. In fact, it was fairly well kept. This cheered her, but as she neared the door that would lead her to the fields that her husband now worked, Molly's nervousness returned.

She stepped into the sunlight and glanced around, noting the well-tended garden, but also the numerous saddles with different brands and the arrows stuck in the trees. And there, leaning on a fencepost, was Lily, her arms lazily sprawled across the board, her eyes silently appraising.

"Hello," she said, her voice neutral, but ever threatening. "Peter's not here."

"Oh, I'm not . . ." she paused, puzzled. "Where is he?"

"Practising."

"Practising what?"

"Fighting." Lily's expression didn't change. "He is an outlaw. That means having to be able to defend himself. Not necessarily having to, but having to be able to."

Molly nodded, twirling her wedding ring around her finger. "Well, I'm here to see you, not Peter."

"Oh," Lily stood up, walking towards her with unhurried steps. "This isn't a social call, I presume."

"No. It's . . ." she hesitated, "financial."

Lily shrugged silently, but she stopped walking, standing at a distance from the other woman. Molly bit her lip, unsure of quite how to approach this strange girl.

"I was, well, thank you for the money you do give us."

"Peter gives it to you. It is his share and he can do what he likes with it."

"But you get it for him." Silence. "In any case, I would, I would, like a bit more, if you don't mind."

"Mind? Why should I mind! It's not like I work for it! It's not like it's actually my money!"

"You're purposely taking it wrong!" Molly cried. "I know you work hard, even risk your life for that money, but I still need more."

A sudden frown washed over Lily's face.

"Is Anna sick? Is that what's wrong?"

"No!" Molly assured her. "She's fine. It's . . . it's my neighbour."

"I don't understand."

"She takes care of Anna sometimes, a very nice older lady, but she's poor and old and sick, you see." Her voice dropped. "I've been giving money to her."

"What!" Lily leapt up. "Peter gives you just enough as it is! I know, because we only take that much! How do you expect to feed yourself, to feed Anna, if you give it away?"

"That's why I came to you! I'm hungry again, and I don't like it, but others are hungrier! Why should I be the only one fed?" She stopped, startled at herself, at the anger in her words, at this sudden outburst towards this girl who was practically a stranger to her. Lily was silent. When she did speak, her voice was low.

"I'd forgotten that hunger. I tried to forget it." She glanced up at Molly. "Are many still hungry?"

"Everyone's still hungry."

"Then I'll get the money." She moved away, picking up her things from the stable doorway and turning them over in her hands.

"How much?" Molly asked, watching as Lily buckled her belt and slid her sword into the scabbard. She picked up her bow and grinned suddenly, adventure growing in her eyes.

"Until I get tired." She laughed suddenly. "Don't be surprised. I like danger. Does that shock you? I'm a thief because I want to be one and I need to be one."

"Lily, I didn't mean . . ."

She shook her head. "Molly, if what I do upsets you, don't think about it. Besides, I like it." Molly twisted her dress in her hands, frowning. Lily shrugged. "I'll get the money, so don't worry. Who cares where it comes from?"

And with that, she rode away.

Edward

Peter moved carefully through the village, cautious, but not really afraid, for he knew almost everyone there. They were almost all farmers like himself and, like him, they felt hunger and desperation. He had no doubt that many had committed the same crime that he had. He had no fear that they would turn him in.

"Peter!" A voice called out. He turned and saw Edward, a neighbouring farmer, approaching him. The other man grabbed hold of Peter's arm, steering him carefully and talking softly under his breath.

"Many families have received some money from your wife, you realize."

Peter was silent. Edward waited for a reply, then continued when he saw none was forthcoming.

"In these times such charity is greatly appreciated. I too am hungry."

Peter stopped him. "If you are asking for money, no. We are not enough of a force to donate to every one. The families come first. You have no family."

"I realize that. What I have heard of your new life is what interests me." Edward paused. "You are living free."

"In a sense. I am a wanted man."

"It is worse to be unwanted!"

"Get on with it."

Edward dropped his voice. "I have no family, as you have said. I have nothing of importance to me here, but I am angry and I am hungry. I want to help you."

"Help me?"

"In your cause. To help the poor." His eyes were eager. "I have considered this carefully. This is what I want."

"Oh." Peter looked at the man. He liked Edward and regretted his suspicions, for he knew the man and his reputation well. Edward was a bright and able man, honest and hard working and forever loyal. Would Lily see that in him, Peter wondered.

"I do not live alone," Peter said.

"Of course not. There are others of course.."

"One other."

"Of course. A leader, perhaps?"

Peter nodded.

"Will he accept me?"

"Well, you've gone right to the point. I have no idea. Perhaps. Would you resent being blindfolded?"

Edward shook his head.

"Then maybe I can arrange a meeting."

*****

It wasn't much later in the day when Peter pushed the blindfolded man gently in front of him into the cave. Carefully he removed the scarf from Edward's eyes.

"Well, this is it," he grinned. "Home sweet home."

"Why are you whispering?" Edward asked.

"Never mind. No one's here."

"You know, if your leader is a thief, which I assume he is, then whispering would do little good. A good thief could hear the footsteps."

Peter grinned. "I know. I'm surprised you realized that."

Edward shrugged and they sat down, waiting. "What is he like? Is he a real thief? I mean a practised one, a good one? What does he look like?"

"Not what you'd expect."

Just then, they heard the sound of a horse neighing. Edward jumped, then grinned self-consciously. "A horse."

"Yes. It is that."

They subsided into silence again. Finally, the door creaked open. There were no footsteps. Then a voice split the air.

"Peter? You're back soon."

Lily slipped into the room, then stopped. She

and Edward locked gazes, both astonished. Peter saw her through Edward's eyes for a moment, a slight girl wearing a white shirt that was too big for her and dark pants, also too big. She had rolled up the sleeves of the shirt and knotted them and had tied a belt around her waist to secure the pants. The only similarity to the outlaw leader that Edward had probably imagined was the sword that hung from this belt and the rage that gleamed in her eyes. Lily was the first to speak.

"What is this?" she snorted. "Who are you? Peter, what is he doing here, who is he and why are you here and not at your other home? Do you want to kill us both?"

Peter gulped, watching her hands as they edged to her knife. He slid his body between her and Edward, talking quickly.

"Lily, this is Edward. I brought him here. He wants to help us. I brought him here instead of going home and no, I do not want to kill us both. He is not a danger. Calm down!"

Her hand stayed on the knife, her eyes on Edward. "Stop staring at me. You have three minutes to convince me why I should not cut you up and feed you to the dog!"

Edward swallowed hard. "Would you really do that?"

She didn't blink. "You're wasting precious time."

"I want to help you."

"Why?"

"Because it's a noble cause."

"It's death. People die doing this!"

"So what?" Edward shrugged. "There's no one to miss me."

Lily watched him, her eyes careful, calm now."How come you have no family?"

"I don't know. I just don't."

Her hand left her knife. She walked across the hall, then back, and stopped. "You can stay, for now, but one false move and you're out of here, whether because I kick you out or because you die." She shrugged. "Mistakes kill, especially on this job."

Five Years Pass

A Day's Work

Peter raised his head from his work, looking over the just-plowed fields of a sickly peasant farmer. It was neither weariness nor hunger that halted Peter's work and, around him, other men also froze. Their nostrils filled with the familiar smell of smoke and they looked to Peter.

Somewhere in the distance Peter heard a yell and Tristan stumbled out of the forest that edged the field. He had joined soon after Edward, those many years ago and the sight of him increased Peter's fear, for in the boy's face was terror.

"Hurry!" he cried. "The sheriff is killing them!"

Peter jumped up, as did the rest of the outlaws. They ran hard towards the distant cluster of houses, their eyes on the pillars of smoke, their swords drawn.

They drew close to the village quickly. It was nothing more than a scattered set of thatched houses, but their straw now danced with fire that leapt from one rooftop to the next. People and livestock swerved in and out between each other and the buildings. The dark horses that carried the sheriff's soldiers strode throughout.

The leader of the soldiers watched the approaching outlaws, then called his marauding troop to retreat. They urged their horses back toward Nottingham, their loot tucked under their saddles. Seeing the fleeing soldiers, the outlaws slowed, reaching the village at a solemn walk.

Lily crouched in the dirt in the center of a small crowd. A woman wailed and the others crept closer to her, their voices a hum of comforting words. Peter stopped, recognizing the grief, then he crept closer. The other men stopped, lingering in the background, unsure of what to do.

"Lily?" Peter whispered, but she did not look up. Her swift fingers were soft as they moved over the small body at her feet, smoothing the boy's clothing, touching his hair and closing his eyes . . . forever. Straightening her shoulders, she moved away, her head bowed. Peter put his arm around her, leading her away as Edward picked up the child and took him into the house.

"What happened?" Peter whispered as they moved back towards Sherwood. Lily didn't look up.

"They were looking for some men, Robin Hood's men. They weren't here, Peter! They never were."

"How do you know that? They could have been here. People know the risks they are taking when they take those men in!"

Lily shook her head. "No. They weren't here. The villagers would know the Merry Men if they had come before. But, Peter, they think we are Robin Hood's!"

She pushed his arm away, turning back to the village.

"Where are you going?"

"They need a grave dug," she said without turning her head. Silently, Tristan and Edward fell into step behind her, picking up the spades discarded along the street. No one said a word.

The Dream

In the dream it was night. In the dream she walked over damp grass in her bare feet. In the dream she came to a river. In the dream she slipped and she was falling, falling, and two long arms grasped her, dead arms, clinging to her, coming out of the water for her, until someone tossed her a rope. She held it tight, but the water went over her head and she couldn't breathe and she screamed underwater, not making a sound. Someone jerked the rope hard, jarring her teeth, and she landed on the river bank, wet and gasping. There was a boy holding the rope, his face white, his hair dark blond, his eyes wide. He called her name, but she ran, and ran, and ran. Someone cried. It was the boy, screaming in pain, begging for her help, but she couldn't. They wrapped him in a cloth and locked him in a coffin, and he cried her name again. And she leapt on the coffin, hammering it, but the wood didn't crack. He was choking, she knew, and she couldn't breathe, and the hammering rang in her ears, until the coffin split open, and she saw him, his eyes open, staring, and she shook him, hard, crying his name, but she didn't know his name, screaming a name she didn't know, until it rang in her ears and she fell crying to the ground.

Lily sat up with a jerk, her nightshirt sticking to her with a cold sweat. An owl hooted, and she jumped, casting a suspicious glance around her room, then calming at the dim outline of familiar furniture. She ran a hand through her hair, pulling the damp strands out of her face.

"A dream. It was only a dream." She pushed aside her blanket and draped her legs over the side of the bed, onto the cold floor, before moving noiselessly out the door and down the stairs.

The night air was cold, especially here in the hallway, but it cooled her feverish face. The dream had almost left her mind, leaving only a vague bitterness behind. She pushed open the outside door and stood in front of it, the view calming her. Someone upstairs was snoring and, for some reason it comforted her, knowing that everyone who had wandered here was still close by. Still, the boy's face lurked in the back of her mind, strangely familiar.

Something furry curled around her legs and she smiled, picking the cat up and breathing in the scent of its fur. Fangs purred loudly, opening its golden eyes, locking gazes with its mistress, and the eyes were so intelligent that Lily almost expected the cat to speak.

"You okay?" She jumped at the voice, then nodded. "Yeah. I guess."

Peter frowned at her softly.

"One of those dreams again?"

"Yeah." She dropped Fangs to the floor and shooed her away, but the movement did not distract Peter as she had hoped it would.

"You screamed, not very loudly, but a scream none the less."

"It was nothing. I don't even remember it anymore." She pulled her nightshirt tighter around her and smiled. "You worry too much."

"I know." He paused. "You can't let things get to you like this."

"Look Peter, I've seen people die before. That had nothing to do with this."

"There was nothing you could have done."

She nodded, but he knew she didn't believe him.

"You staying up?"

She nodded again. "I'm fine, Peter. Go to bed."

He shrugged, kissed the top of her head, and returned to his room.

"Goodnight."

She didn't answer, oblivious to him, and so he left her there, alone in the doorway, listening to the night sounds, where unknown names did not lurk to trouble her.

Robing Robin

The next day, in the same small village, a girl sat spinning, her usual song quieted. Her fingers skipped over the wool and the hum of the spinning wheel blocked out all other noise. As a shadow fell across her work, she paused but did not look up.

"Why have you returned? There is nothing left to take!" Her voice shook as she whirled around. "Have you not done enough already?"

The figure standing before her stepped back, not the merciless soldier she'd expected, but only another girl.

"I'm sorry. Have I come too soon?" She glanced back at the door as though wanting to run from the house.

"No," the spinner replied. "It may be too late. Whom do you seek?"

"You don't know me. I was here yesterday . . ."

The spinner peered inside the hood, but the other shrank back.

"You buried my brother," the spinner said.

"I buried a boy," the visitor replied.

"You are one of the outlaws!"

The visitor nodded. "I'm sorry to scare you."

"No. Forgive my rudeness. I did not realize that you came from Robin Hood. Will you give him our thanks?"

"But he did not help you!"

The spinner frowned, shaking her head. "My brother died, but more could have if Robin Hood's men had not scared the soldiers away. And you helped us bury him, and pick up what was left of our belongings. I do not expect a miracle. Please, give him my thanks."

The strange girl frowned, but nodded. "I will."

*****

Lily left the house hurriedly. It reminded her too much of yesterday. The burnt houses still spoke of fires and the pitiful grave spoke of the sheriff's "justice." She had dug that grave. Some dirt still clung to her cape. Leaping on Starline, she nervously unlaced the moneybag from her belt and dropped it on the spinner's doorstep. Kicking her heels into the horse, Lily sped away, not slowing until she reached the shelter of Sherwood Forest.

Starline slowed, his feet lifting up small clouds of dust. Lily kept her head bent low, her eyes on her hands. Where had the Merry Men been as she buried that child? Were they too busy being heroes? Her hand tightened angrily around the knife tied to her leg without her even realizing that she did so.

And so, when the bushes rustled nearby, Lily tensed, her heart beating faster. She knew the sound of footsteps meant for silence. She knew how thieves walked and she knew that these were not her thieves. They were Robin Hood's. The hand around the knife tensed.

"Halt!" The voice rang out clearly, echoing off the trees and clouding her mind. She shook it off, forcing herself free from memories. Instead, she watched the men. They were not going to attack. She could tell.

"Please, Milady," one young man called out to her in the same disorienting voice. He was handsome, with shaggy brown hair showing beneath his cap and careful grey-blue eyes that watched her every movement. "Please. A small toll."

Lily almost laughed at the gentlemanly tone, the polite question that was so unlike her own style.

"Why don't you just take it?"

"We'd rather make it easy for you." He laughed then. "But I assure you that we will take your money if it is not given to us."

"Easier for me?" she asked. "If you think you

can, then come and take it."

With a shrug, he stepped up to her, but he kept his hand on his knife. With a mock bow, he held out his hand. "The gold, please."

Instead, Lily took the hand and swung the man around so that he was against Starline and her dagger was at his throat.

"You stupid man," she said, her light fingers wandering almost automatically to his belt, where she knew his purse would be. Her fingers untied it carefully and her smile grew into a dangerous grin.

"What are you doing?" he protested. She pressed the knife against his neck.

"Haven't you been robbed before?" she asked, her fingers pulling out his sword and slipping it under her cape. "Do you have anything else?"

"No."

"I thought not."

"Milady, you do realize that I am one of Robin Hood's men? You are robbing a thief!"

Here her face broke into a complete and delighted grin. "You started it."

"Milady," another man said, stepping forward. "We apologize. Release him and be on your way."

"Sir, I did not ask to be robbed. I did not ask you to involve yourselves with me. It was your decision."

"Will, are you all right?" The man turned to

the captive.

"As well as can be expected." Will tried to smile with his reply, but the knife restricted his movements.

The speaker turned back to Lily. "What do you want? It is not even his money. You steal from the poor."

Lily's fingers tightened on the knife. "At least I fight for them. You leave them to die, to carry the blame for your deeds. The sheriff slaughters them in your name."

The man turned away, pulling down his hood and rubbing his blue eyes. These no longer danced, but were suddenly sad.

Will felt the knife at his throat slip, the fingers loosen suddenly and the girl draw a sharp breath. Taking advantage of her distraction, he grabbed her arm and pulled her from her horse. She fell sharply on the ground, the knife clattering beside her. Instantly, she was on her feet again, an instinctive gesture. Her gaze was locked on Robin's face.

"Robin?" The voice was soft and quavering, unbelieving. Then, she suddenly whirled around and leapt onto the stallion, not bothering to pick up her loot. The animal sped away in the opposite direction, with the girl bent low over its mane. Will stepped forward to retrieve his things, rubbing his neck.

Will

One Dead Forester

Lily moved silently over the forest floor, her feet making no sound. Her every movement faded into the forest noises. She was as much a part of the forest as the trees and it kept her secrets. Now, as she moved quietly among the foliage, even the thieves ahead of her were unaware of Lily.

She was unsure of why she followed them, why she was drawn to them, even of what had happened to her on the way back from the village those many weeks ago when they had confronted her. She no longer questioned this urge to learn more about these men. She just obeyed, keeping her eyes open for the Merry Men and then following them, as she did now.

Robin's men paused, walked in circles for a moment and settled down. She slid into the underbrush around them. It was only when they slipped into the forest around the cave that she followed them. Their affairs at home or abroad were no business of hers. She respected their privacy that much, but when they crossed into the deeper part of the forest, away from their own camp, they walked into her world, and she watched them and silently learned their names.

Today it was a small group, and she knew all of them. The fair-haired boy was Alan O'Dell, a musician of some kind, and the youngest there. Beside him was Much, eating a chunk of bread. The third's face always haunted her for days after seeing him. It was a handsome and friendly face, with eyes that had mischief beneath their blue, tanned skin and honey-coloured hair and light beard. His name was Robin and Lily knew very well that he was Robin Hood, but she really didn't care. The stories didn't impress her. He was more cautious than the others, watching the surrounding woods with a careful eye, which made Lily laugh silently. She was invisible to him.

Will Scarlett was the name of the last, the one she had robbed on the road. She liked him, for he was friendly and had a pleasant face. She did not forget his politeness on the road, his apologetic manner. It endeared him to her in a small way, his attitude so different from the rough world she knew. His eyes were hazel and he had brown hair. What Lily liked about him most was the air of satisfaction he carried about him, unlike the restless masses she knew inhabited the countryside. It was something she lacked.

Their talk did not interest her. It was idle talk made over a meal and meaningless to her. Soon she listened with only one ear, bored with this excursion. Her other ear automatically picked through the forest sounds and heard twigs breaking, the bushes rustling and brushing against cloth. She lay still, moving only to draw her bow and notch an arrow to it.

The Forester Lily had been following with her eyes now leapt into the clearing and made a low, strangled sound as the arrow sank into his heart, staining his uniform with dark blood. The four outlaws leapt up, confused by the man and his death. Then, five more Foresters leapt from the brush and there was no time for questions.

Lily did nothing more now, but only sat, and watched. It was a battle, not an unfair attack, and it was their battle. She watched, her bow silent, as the Foresters fled. Lily let them go by, so close that she felt a breeze as they passed. Then she stood, gathered her arrows and left.

Will

Robin nudged the dead man with his foot, puzzled at the arrow jutting from his chest, red as the very blood it spilt. None he knew used the colour red on their arrows, which meant that the archer was a stranger. The colour of an arrow's feather was a badge of its owner, but this one he had never seen. Robin was worried. Firstly, this stranger had watched them, without fear, or need of it. He had been able to go undetected. Secondly, the Foresters had done almost as good a job as the stranger in terms of invisibility.

Robin looked at his comrades and opened his mouth to speak. Then his eyes scanned the circle. He stopped.

"Where's Will?"

*****

Will's eyes searched the forest and saw a broken twig.

"Not so invisible, are you?" he murmured, following the almost non-existent trail. It was hard to follow, but he could see that it led to the river's edge. There he paused, hesitant.

The river was easily crossed, he knew. Here, the water reached only a little past his ankles. However, the other side of the river was known, by the Merry Men, to be haunted. The outside world might or might not believe that. Will did not know or care, for the outlaws knew that there were two theories that were held by the outside world about the hauntings. One, widely supported by the outsiders, was that the Merry Men were haunting the far shore, using tricks to keep people away. Of course, Will knew this one to be untrue and so he had to lean towards the other. The part of the forest across the river was indeed haunted.

He crossed. Ghosts or no, he wanted to meet the man who had saved them. At the opposite bank, he stepped onto dry grass and looked around. The few clues that had led him this far had been hard enough to follow, but now it seemed that the archer had disappeared without a trace. Will frowned, but continued walking, his slow stride covering much of the forest floor easily, but there was no sign of the archer.

Something howled nearby, too near. Will quickened his pace toward the road and placed his hand on his sword, but the howling stopped suddenly.

There was only silence. Silence, a snap and he was lifted by a sort of springboard that flung him into the air and toward Sherwood Road.

Will met the road in a ball, rolling with the impact, the wind knocked out of him. Above him stood a troop of horses with the sheriff at their head. Will looked up at them, meeting the sheriff's shocked gaze and then, leaping to his feet, he raced into the forest once again.

Will ran only a little way. He could already hear the soldiers giving chase. He dived onto his belly among the protective leaves of a huddle of bushes and waited, grass tickling his skin. There was nowhere to run, so why bother? He'd only lead them back to the camp if he ran there.

The horses were in the forest now. Will could hear their breath and the stomping of their hooves close by. These soldiers were a useless lot, turning and stretching their necks, as though hoping he'd jump out screaming "Here I am!"

They were poor riders in the forest, Will noted, laughing at their efforts to maneuver around each other and the trees. One man's horse reeled. Its rider teetered, fell and landed in the dust. He raised his head slowly, spitting out dust and looked directly into the eyes of Will Scarlett.

Will leapt up, sword ready. The blade met flesh only three times and then he was down on the ground, tasting blood in his mouth and feeling ropes on his wrists.

They hauled him into the sunlight, eager for their rightful praise, but the sheriff only glanced at him briefly, smiled and waved him away. Will knew what his enemy was thinking. It was in his eyes. One doesn't speak to dead men.

Prison

Will glanced around the prison without turning his head, taking in every detail, trying to fathom a means of escape. The only thing that came to mind was complete horror. This seemed the very gateway to hell.

The soldiers kicked at one of the creatures that skittered across the floor. Will thought the furry beasts were cats, but when they turned he could see their pointed noses and beady eyes and he was glad when the soldiers locked him in ceiling chains, far from the reaches of the rats.

Will eyed the prison more carefully from his upside-down view. It was a square room of no spectacular size or design, just four stone walls, covered in dirt and blood, both dried and fresh. A steady row of chains ran along the walls and when space had run out, ceiling chains were attached. Inside these scattered pairs of chains were men, although hardly recognizable as such or distinguishable from each other. Each seemed only another skeletal figure in rust-eaten shackles.

However, as time passed Will learned who they were, naming them and categorizing them in his mind.

There, over on the wall was the "crazed one," who had attacked the prisoner beside him and had been moved to a secluded set of chains. He now stared at the ceiling all day, singing wild rhymes, a thin old man, with tangled hair and a few yellow teeth.

The man he had attacked was crazy too, a shorter, calmer version of the other, although he tended to shriek loudly at night, screaming of battles and monsters. Then there was Charles, who was about Will's own age, with wild eyes and blond hair, a man desperate to remain sane. Will did not know if this was working, for Charles sat in the corner now, muttering. "Stupid! Why Charles?" and then, "God, don't let them come. Don't let them come. Sorry, sorry, sorry," until he finally fell silent, too tired to continue his monologue.

And there were so many more, coming and going before Will's eyes, but they faded away as time blurred into an endless train of tortures. Will's body was burned and cut and his wrists were rubbed raw from the shackles. His was a world of upside-down views. The other prisoners disappeared and the room disappeared, all pushed aside by the dull pain that emanated throughout his entire body. The mutterings and screams of the chained men around him were only a faint buzz to Will. He no longer knew when one died or a new one was brought in. They were all the same and he was tired.

Time passed, unrecorded, and then one day, the sheriff remembered him. The chains fell away, and Will was dragged off, not to the torture chambers, but down a long hall. His knees hurt from dragging, but his legs just wouldn't work, and so he let them drag him, four broad-shouldered guards escorting one lone, undernourished, battered, immobile, unarmed man towards whatever fate they had decided for him.

Bargains

Robert de Rainault, the Sheriff of Nottingham, smiled to himself, lounging on the throne he had erected, surrounded by rich tapestries and silks, and dozens of women who had no choice but to obey his every whim. Luxury. He breathed it in, lived on it, feeding only that and his power. It was almost perfect, except that Robin Hood still mocked his power. But that would end soon enough.

He glanced down the length of the enormous room, empty except for the throne and the tables and women around him. The rest of the room stood elegantly unfurnished, which only drew attention to the beautiful tapestries that hung on the wall, from ceiling to floor, and the purple carpet leading from the throne to the door.

There was a practical purpose to the emptiness, for even everyday objects could easily serve as weapons in the hands of desperate people, and the people who surrounded him were often desperate and driven by hate. The sheriff smiled again at the thought of the hate he could drive into people. What power!

The doors at the far end of the room opened and two guards walked in, a limp form between them. Will Scarlett was hardly recognizable, his clothes nothing but strands of cloth now, his cheeks and eyes were sunken, his hair was long and shaggy, hanging in a stringy mass around his face. The guards released him and he almost fell, but at the last moment he pulled himself up tall and stepped forward. His eyes burned in his shadowy eye sockets and a shiver of fear ran down the sheriff's back.

"Get out!" the sheriff ordered the women and they leapt up, awakened from the trance Will Scarlett had cast over them all. They scurried away like beaten puppies, only the bravest daring to glance up at Will as they passed by, their eyes drawn to the pain and hate in his face.

As the door shut behind the women, Will began to move, his steps slow and deliberate, filled with effort. Just as he reached the throne one of the guards grabbed his arms. This time Will did not slump against them. He stayed standing, trying hard not to fall to his knees.

The sheriff stood up, circling Will, curling his lip. He adored elegance and cleanliness. This pathetic creature nauseated him. He stepped back, out of range of the putrid smell of the prisons.

"Do you know why I hate you, Scarlett?" he asked suddenly. "It's because you don't appreciate fine things. My rule here is a fine thing. My power is a fine thing. My wealth is a fine thing. I like it. I like money, Scarlett. It is convenient. It buys you anything in the world."

"Happiness?" Will whispered through dry lips.

"Yes. You see, it's not the money I crave, but the power it buys. That's the beauty."

The sheriff laughed, lifting a goblet from the hands of a nearby servant and bringing it to his lips, swallowing. Will licked his dried lips and tried not to watch.

"You're not too dangerous," the sheriff said. "Compared to some, I mean." He ran his finger around the rim of the goblet carefully. "I'd be willing to exchange one life for another."

"Whose?' Will muttered, though he knew the answer. He tried not to watch the goblet, tried to think of anything but the dryness in his throat. It was next to impossible.

"Robin Hood's life for yours." The sheriff stepped forward, lowering the goblet to the level of Will's lips. "Shall we drink on it?"

He watched the outlaw's eyes, watched them glance around the room, judging an escape, then eyeing the goblet. His tongue flicked out and the sheriff dared to hope. Then Will brought his chin up suddenly, knocking the goblet away from him.

Red wine splashed out onto the sheriff, spreading over his clothes slowly.

"You will be defeated some day," Will warned coldly. Fear leapt for a minute in the sheriff's heart, then it returned to stone.

"You are not in the position to be making threats. Now you will pay for this insult." He stepped away, waving his hand at the proud prisoner. "Beat him. Take him back to the prison. Wait until he awakes and then kill him."

Refilling the goblet, the sheriff turned to watch, a cool smile on his face, as Will Scarlett disappeared under a battering of fists and whips, falling heavily to the floor, groaning in his efforts not to scream.

*****

Two of the guards were left with the job of carrying Will Scarlett's limp body back to the dungeon and to his chains. They carried him between them, swinging him wildly and laughing.

"For a great fighter, he's not so heavy," one laughed as they carried him around the corner of the building.

"Nay. He's not great. If he was, he wouldn't be here."

"Bring him here!" the new voice startled them. They looked up at another man, his gold hair almost hidden under his helmet, his uniform a bit snug. He stood before a large cart filled with the corpses of dead prisoners.

"He ain't dead yet."

The new guard snorted. "I know that, but he's being moved to another dungeon, so no one can break in and get him out. I doubt he'll mind riding in this."

"I never heard nothing about no move!"

The stranger pulled himself up to his full height, and he towered over them. " 'Tain't my problem. I got's the orders right here."

The guards with Will glanced at the paper with its meaningless letters and shrugged. "Well, I recognize the seal all right. 'Tis the sheriff's. Are you sure 'bout this?"

The stranger nodded. "Would I lie to ye? Come on! We're wastin' time!" He whirled around. "Boy, help these men! Get your arse in gear!"

The slight driver of the cart leapt up and raced around to help. They heaved the limp body on top of the others and then the driver returned to his seat. The guards stepped back, unsure.

"Think we should check and see if it's all right?"

"I don't have the time," the other roared. "Now, get back to your posts!"

They hurriedly obeyed, disappearing inside the dungeon. The strange guard leapt into the wagon, pushing the awakening "corpses" back down with a warning.

"Hurry up, Lil," he urged the driver as she clicked the reins. "We don't have much time!"

"I know, Peter!" she returned as the horse broke into a gallop. "And don't yell at me anymore, boy." She drew out the last word, laughing as they fled through the gates.

Meeting

Will opened his eyes slowly, warily. It wouldn't do for him to look awake in this dungeon. They treat you better when they want you alive and think you're dying.

The light here hurt his eyes. Why was it so bright? He quickly closed them and tried instead to listen to the sounds he heard, but they blended together, refusing to cooperate with his efforts.

When he opened his eyes again Will was ready for the light. After a momentary blindness, he realized that it was sunlight, streaming through a window directly onto his face. He sat up and looked around.

The room was clean and empty of any other people. There was, however, a mattress on the floor by the bed he was in and on it was crumpled a pile of clothes. Besides that, there was a chair, a wash basin and a large trunk at the foot of the bed. The wash basin had water in it, and so Will staggered to it and splashed some on his face. The cool water slid over his bare skin and he drank some from his cupped hands.

On the chair was a folded shirt, not new, but clean. Will slipped this over his freshly bandaged chest and walked out the open door, down a set of stairs and out the door beside them.

The sight of the trees that encircled the glade was so welcome that, for a moment, Will just stood and looked at them, not caring if his host found him in so vulnerable a position and decided to get rid of a possibly unwanted guest.

Finally, he turned and viewed the rest of his surroundings. To his left was a faithfully weeded garden. To his right was a pasture, with a dark horse in its far corner. Paths were beaten into the rest of the ground, twisting here, there and away again. The only sound was water splashing in the distance and his own breathing.

When the splashing stopped suddenly, he froze. There was no sound at all, unnaturally so. Will stepped back as silence screamed in his ears. Something soft was under his foot, and he tripped. Will found himself with his face in the dirt, tasting blood and soil in his mouth. Something yowled angrily at his feet and he slowly looked down at it.

The cat was enormous, a cascade of golden fur over taut muscles. She licked her tail indignantly and glowered at the man who had tripped over her. Her yellow eyes narrowed, her lips pulled back, as did her ears, and a set of glistening fangs were exposed to view.

Will staggered to his feet and backed away. Instantly, a knife point took position behind his ear and a hand was pressed against his lower back.

"Go." He began to move. "Not you! Fangs."

The cat stood, stretched and slunk away, her tail lashing sulkily.

"Turn around." He obeyed and the knife followed, to rest under his chin.

"Oh. It's you." His captor lowered the dagger, glared at him and then replaced the blade in her belt. Her dark hair was wet, falling in thick waves down her back. The eyes that watched him were dark and wary.

"What are you staring at?" she demanded.

"You're beautiful!" Will stopped as her hand moved. He somehow knew that she would stick her knife between his ribs without hesitation, but she only ran her hand through her hair and pulled it away from her face.

"You brought me up here to tell me that?"

"Where were you?"

"Bathing. I was taking advantage of what was supposed to be empty grounds." She grinned and took his hand in a firm handshake, the gesture so alien in a woman that he almost pulled away. "I'm Lily."

"Will." He gazed at her again. What was it about

her that seemed so familiar? He carefully scrutinized her face, but could not pinpoint what it was that he recognized.

"Nice to officially meet you." She lowered her voice. "Are you feeling much better now?"

"Oh. Yes."

"Good. When we got you out of that dreadful prison, you were coughing up all sorts of unpleasant stuff. We had to move you to my room so that someone could keep an eye on you. You weren't a very good roommate." She laughed, then turned to call to the two men who had just come into the yard.

"There you are! You two! Show Will here around. Is everyone else back too?" She raced towards the stable, calling back to him over her shoulder. "I'll talk to you soon. We have to discuss moving you to another room."

Will nodded, and she was gone, leaving him in the less desirable company of his two guides. The men laughed as they followed his gaze, recognizing the look.

"An unwise woman to set your sight on," one chuckled. "Ask anyone here. She won't even notice you."

He and his companion laughed, leading Will away. The two woodsmen were loyal to their orders, spending the remainder of the day singing the praises of their home and leading Will over every inch of it. As darkness fell, they returned to the cave and led Will into a new room, where he fell exhausted into bed.

Dreaming

Will sat up in his bed, waking from his sleep in confusion. It was cool here at night, and now someone whimpered in the distance. He walked down the hallway, following the sound, and eventually found himself in front of Lily's room.

Lily was curled up in a ball, her small body making her look like a child in Peter's arms. She was still asleep, and it was her crying Will had heard. Peter was stroking her hair softly, waiting patiently for her to awake. When he saw Will he glared at him, the grey eyes under the gold hair suddenly terrifying.

"Get out," he hissed. Will turned and left, walking outside. Under the dark sky, he couldn't hear the cries of this woman-child, and soon fell asleep.

*****

"About time you woke up." The cold voice seemed

to come from nowhere. Will sat up and looked around.

He was still outside, but now it was daylight and Lily sat on a stone close by, carefully cutting slices off an apple, and eating them, piece by piece. She did not smile.

"Peter said I had another one of my dreams last night. He says you were there." He nodded and she looked away.

"You don't like to seem weak, do you?"

She lifted her head, and her eyes burned. "You don't know anything about it!"

"Dreams don't make you weak."

"Listen, Will Scarlett! You may think that you know me, but you don't! You do not know what goes on inside my head!"

He shrugged. "I just figured you'd have to be twice as tough as everybody else to get any respect."

She stared at the trees, pulling hair out of her eyes. "It comes with the territory."

"Are they bad? The dreams?" She was silent, then nodded. "Do they happen often?"

She shrugged. "Often enough. You won't say anything will you?"

"No. But I'm worried about this fear of weakness in you."

"Weakness is conquered. To be weak is to die."

"So, it's all about death."

"No. It's about living." She looked up at him. "You don't understand me. I suggest you stop trying." With an odd, crooked smile on her face, she ended the conversation. Will stood for a moment, uncomfortable, unsure of what to do. Eventually, he retreated to the cave.

Target Practice

Will loosed another arrow at the target at the far side of the glade. The arrow flew true, hitting the center of the bullseye. Will let out a yell of pleasure.

"It's easy to hit a piece of wood that just stands there and doesn't move."

"Didn't see you there, Lily." Will wasn't surprised. She often walked about without a sound and no one could tell when she passed. Now she sat on a log beside him and her words rang like a challenge in his ears.

"Can you do better?"

"I can shoot a Forester through the heart before he has time to strike a blow."

"What did you say?" He turned on her slowly.

"Your hearing's fine. I'll not repeat myself for you!" She doodled in the dirt with a twig and ignored him.

"Lily, what did you mean by that? About the Forester?"

"Nothing in particular."

Will thrust the bow at her. “Shoot.”

“No.”

“Shoot.”

“No.” But she was smiling and he grew more convinced with every second that passed that it had been she who had killed that Forester those many weeks before, the Forester who would have killed Robin or Alan or Much or himself.

“Lily, shoot. I want to see.”

She didn’t take her eyes off his face, just grabbed the bow, fit one of her own arrows to it and fired, never looking at the target. Will turned to the bullseye.

“Fair shot,” Lily said behind him and it was. The arrow had reached the bullseye at an angle, but it was still lodged in the center of the bullseye. The thin shaft swayed from the force of its flight and the blood-red feathers moved dizzyingly before Will’s eyes.

Lil

Will lounged in the empty cave, scratching Fang's belly. He had already mucked out the stable, brushed his horse, cleaned his one set of clothes, shone his sword, practised fighting and shooting and he'd found a book among one of the piles of loot. He'd spent a full hour trying to understand what the title said, but the only letters he knew were his initials, W and S, and neither was in the book's title.

Not one of the thieves was back yet. He wanted to be out there tonight, fighting and robbing and contributing in some way to the cause, but he was stuck waiting another week before he could set foot outside the cave. The trial period of two weeks was much slacker than the Merry Men's one of a month and a half, but it still drove Will to distraction.

He heard footsteps pounding through the forest. Leaping up, he ran to the door and flung it open.

"Where's everyone else?" he asked as Lily and

the man he remembered as Peter raced past him. Peter kept going, but Lily stopped.

"It's Peter's wife, Molly! The baby's coming! We have to go! You, too! And get your sword! And saddle the horses! We'll have to stand guard! Move!" It was a fast tumble of words, but Will made it out. He raced to the stable and tacked up three horses in the time it usually took to saddle just one. No sooner was he done than Peter and Lily appeared beside him, their faces flushed.

"Let's go!"

Will crouched down in the saddle, urging his horse onward, rain beating against his face. He could see the shadowy figures beside him, also racing, and he let them guide him. The trees grew scarcer and then a house appeared before them. The horses slowed, then stopped. Peter leapt off and raced inside.

Lily took the reins of Peter's horse and calmly turned it towards the lean-to, her steps leisurely. Will stared at her.

"Aren't you going to go in?"

"Oh, no. Have you ever been in there? It's just a small hut. If you and I went in, it would probably fall apart." She smiled nervously, looping the reins around a post and sitting down on the rickety bench in front of the cottage.

"Sit," she said.

He obeyed, and they sat in silence. He watched

Lily stare at the sky. Her lips moved as she counted the stars. And then she stopped.

"This will be Peter's second child." She smiled. "You know, most people desperately want a son, but Peter doesn't seem to care about that."

"My parents desperately wanted a son," Will said. There was silence.

"I must have been a bit of a disappointment," Lily murmured. Will said nothing. They sat through a much longer silence. Lily glanced towards the door nervously.

"I hope she's doing well." Lily's words were calm, but her voice shook.

"Relax. Women have been doing this since Eve."

"Who?" Lily's eyes were puzzled.

"The first woman."

"Oh, yes. Peter told me that story once."

Will stared at her for a moment, then looked away. "She'll be fine."

"Are you married? Do you have children?" Lily asked, challenging this statement.

"No."

"Then how do you know if she is fine?" Lily stopped. "I get defensive when I'm nervous."

"I don't mind."

"And you're right." She nodded furiously to herself. "Molly's going to be fine."

"Of course."

They waited some more, glancing at the door

anxiously. Lily twirled her knife in her hands, then put it back in her belt, then pulled it out again.

"Stop fidgeting."

"Sorry."

Just then a howl went up inside the shack. Lily jumped up, her eyes darting everywhere.

"It's the baby!" She grabbed Will's hand and pulled him towards the door. "Come on!"

"I don't even know them!" Will objected, but she ignored him. "Lily, wait until the midwife leaves. You said the place was too small for us."

She stopped. "You're right. We'll wait."

She returned to waiting, but now she stood at the door, her arms crossed impatiently. The midwife, when she finally left, cast a curious glance at Lily before she raced inside. Will followed.

Molly was asleep, but Peter was awake. He sat in a chair in the corner, cooing softly to the bundle in his arms, an awe on his face that belongs solely to fathers. Lily stopped at the sight, then inched closer. She stood at his elbow and looked into the wrinkled red face.

"She's beautiful."

Peter nodded. "She's the most beautiful baby in the world!" He smiled at Lily. "Do you want to hold her?"

"Do you think I could?" she whispered. He nodded and slid the bundle into her arms, arranging her hand to cradle the little head. She smiled softly, biting her lip.

"Hi," she whispered. "My name's Lily."

The baby didn't move, just kept its eyes closed, clenching its fists tightly. Peter reached out and brushed a rough finger down the newborn cheek.

"That's her name too."

Lily looked up, her face stunned. "You named her Lily?"

"I thought that . . . well . . . yes, if it's fine with you."

"It's perfect with me." Peter grinned at her words, relieved. Lily turned. "Come and see, Will."

Will crept closer, nodding shyly to Peter, then glancing at little Lily. She smacked her lips loudly and scrunched up her face until every wrinkle bent into wrinkles. Will laughed softly.

"I see the resemblance."

"Peter, can Will hold her?" Peter nodded and moved his daughter into Will's arms, gently resting her head against his shirt. Will froze, not daring to breathe, but she didn't cry.

Lily glanced at Peter. "Do you want us to stay and guard the place. We will, if you say so."

"No." He shook his head. "We'll be fine, but you'd better go. We're all tired."

Lily nodded and Will reluctantly relinquished the younger Lily to her father. Then they slipped out the door, leaving Peter to gaze in thankful wonder at his family.

Baptism

About a week later Lily barreled into Will's room in typical style. The door was thrown open and slammed against the wall, waking him with a thunderous bang. He sat up.

"Yes?"

"Hurry up or we're going to be late!"

"What for?" He rubbed his eyes as she hurriedly rooted through his small pile of clothes and threw some at him.

"For the priest!"

"What?" He stood up. "Why are we going to the church?"

"Little Lily is getting baptized today and we're the godparents." She glanced up. "I forgot to tell you."

She dashed out the door and Will followed. "Forgot to tell me?" he wailed. "Good God, Lily!" He stopped. "Why am I a godparent? He hardly knows me."

Lily stopped at a bench and began cleaning her boots furiously. "Peter seems to think you've got a good head on your shoulders. Besides, he said something about it being appropriate, you being at the birth and all." She whirled around. "Why aren't you dressed?"

"I . . ."

"I told you to get dressed! Why aren't you dressed? We are going to be late!"

"Lily!"

"I already said you'd do it, so go."

"Fine!" He started up the stairs. "You owe me one."

"I owe you nothing! It's an honour!"

*****

Lily glanced at the ceiling, her eyes wide. "So this is a church."

"Yes."

"I often wondered what they looked like inside." She slid into the pew nearest to the door, ignoring the rows of empty seats that stretched out before them.

"No. We go up front." Will took her arm and guided her towards the altar where the priest stood. Lily frowned.

"Is it safe?"

Will nodded. "He's christening Lily, isn't he? Obviously, he doesn't quite follow the rules. We're safe here."

"Come to pick a date?" the priest asked, glancing with disapproval at Lily's clothing. He looked up at Will's blank face. "Aren't you the couple come to arrange the wedding?"

Lily laughed loudly. "No!" She didn't even attempt to disguise her mirth, her laughter echoing in the solemn building.

"We're here for the baptism," Will said softly, blushing as Lily tried to control her laughter.

The priest nodded. "Oh. Yes."

"Why are you laughing so hard?" Will snapped to Lily. "It's not that funny."

"Oh, but it is," she gasped.

"Well, control yourself. Peter's here."

Anna slipped down the aisle towards them and proceeded to hide behind Lily's leg and stare at Will a bit nervously. Meanwhile, the priest began to intone the prayers. Lily didn't really listen. She looked at the altar with interest, then hummed a raunchy tune she'd heard somewhere, but she didn't sing the words so the priest seemed to think it a hymn. And then the baby was placed in her arms and she spoke to it in a low voice until the priest coughed loudly.

"Oh!" she started, then repeated the words the priest spoke in a loud, clear tone, but the only words she really heard were the child's name, Lily Eleanor Semmons. Lily turned it around in her mouth and spoke it softly to the baby throughout the rest of the service until Molly came over to reclaim her child.

As they walked home together, Lily smiled at Will. "It's a lovely name isn't it? She's even lovelier."

He nodded, watching her. "Yes. That's true."

"It even looks nice written down. My signature is so abrupt, but hers flows."

"Written down?"

She dug into her pocket, producing a tattered piece of paper. "See. After the birth I wrote it down."

"The name?"

"No! The event! I couldn't get the feeling right, of course. It sounds so bare when you read it." She pressed it into his hands and quickened her step, walking ahead of him now. "You keep it. It's not very good, but her name, oh that's lovely!"

Will stared at the paper in his hand, at the meaningless jumble of letters, then up at Lily's retreating back.

"You can read?"

"Of course! Can't you?"

Will didn't answer. He walked on silently, his hands trembling as they held the paper. Suddenly, he grabbed Lily's arm, pulling her to a halt.

"Lily, you have to tell me who you are."

She stared at him, her smile gone. "What do you mean?"

"Only nobles . . . Peasants can't . . . You can

read!"

"I know." She smiled, a bit nervously. "No one else can. I tried to teach Peter and he's fairly good, but I am a terrible teacher. No patience." She grinned. "Come on! Let's get home quickly!"

"Why?"

"Well, we can't just wander around all day. There's so much to do at home, you know. Rob this person and that person and all. Come on!"

He left it at that and it wasn't until he was lying awake in bed that night that he realized something. She had never answered his question and he was beginning to think she didn't intend to.

Water Falling

"Good Lord, it's hot!" Will ducked under the water again, relieved to lower his body into the coolness. Ever since the baptism two weeks ago, the temperature seemed to have kept climbing. Everyone was lazy and the swimming hole was in constant use. Today, however, only he and Lily were there.

"That looks refreshing," she laughed, splashing him as he came up. Will cocked his eyebrow comically.

"Hypocrite!"

She laughed at this, sitting on the dry shore, her bare feet kicking up more water. "Aren't you hot?"

Lily shrugged. "A bit."

He pulled himself out of the water, grinning. "I will not let you slowly murder yourself out in that heat."

"What do you mean?" she shot at him. "What can you do about it?"

He grinned even wider. "This!" Will swooped

down on her, lifting her from the bank and carrying her steadily out into the water.

"Will . . ." she hissed. "Put me back."

"To die slowly? Never!" Lily's face disappeared against his chest and her hands clenched behind his neck as he continued walking. The water lapped at his back and Lily's waist. She was silent, not even breathing.

"Lily?" he asked. "Are you . . ."

Cold metal came to rest on his neck and Lily finally looked up. Her face was streaked with silent tears, her eyes frightened and desperate. The knife shook in her hand, as her voice did when she spoke.

"Put me back, Will." She swallowed, her hand tightening around the knife. "Please."

Will stared at her, frightened. "What's wrong?"

"Just put me back."

Nodding, he obeyed, slowly moving through the water and back to shore. He set her on the ground and as her feet touched it she let go of him, dropping to the earth of the river bank. The knife still quivered in her hand; her eyes were still fixed on his face. And as their eyes connected, they were both suddenly still. The world grew silent. The knife slipped away and each leaned toward the other. Their lips met.

Lily stepped back suddenly, her eyes dropping to the ground, her hands clenching the knife. She laughed weakly.

"We have to stop meeting at the end of a knife."

Will nodded. "It's becoming a habit." He did not drop his eyes from her face, watching the darting pupils. She had stopped smiling.

"Look, Will," Lily said quietly. "It is very hot. Why don't you go back to swimming? I have some things to do."

He nodded and she turned away, walking uncertainly towards the cave and away from him.

Home

When he awoke the next morning, Will could see Lily pacing across the room. He pretended not to be awake and watched her from under half-closed eyelids. Lily's face was slightly pale, but her cheeks were flushed. Her eyes darted towards him constantly. Then, suddenly she knelt by the bed and gazed at his face solemnly, her dark eyes almost black in her face. Will closed his eyes completely.

Her fingers brushed his lips, but that was all, a slight, nervous touch that was quickly removed. He could hear her dart away. The door closed softly and he opened his eyes. Lily was gone.

He didn't bother looking for her. There was no point to it, for she knew the grounds and forest better than anyone else and could vanish on a whim. He almost wondered if it was a supernatural power she held that she could disappear so well.

And so Will dressed and ate and walked and worked in the garden. There he relaxed, the moist scent of the earth soothing every part of him. Time vanished and when Lily suddenly rode up to him and reined Starline in, he had no idea how much of the day had passed.

Lily looked at Will. "Come with me?"

Silently, he slid into the saddle behind her, his arms around her waist. Starline turned and they trotted through the stable, and out the other side.

Neither spoke. Will leaned against Lily, smelling horses in her hair. She ignored him, her hands gently touching the reins and guiding Starline through the trees, until the sound of running water greeted Will's ears. He sat up straighter, watching as the river that ran through the center of Sherwood came into view. Lily pulled Starline to a halt and turned to Will.

"You get off here," she said. Will glanced at the water and unlaced his arms. He slid off Starline. Lily smiled at him sadly.

"Wouldn't it be fun if I could keep you?" She smiled, then shook her head. "The Merry Men have been looking for you. They miss you." She pursed her lips. "You belong with them, Will. Will Scarlett."

She leaned forward, then seemed to change her mind and sat back in the saddle. Then she kicked her heels into Starline and galloped away, refusing to look back. Will gazed after her, then turned to the other side of the forest. His eyes brightened and his step quickened. He was going home.

*****

"I didn't expect to find you here." Peter watched her, swimming from one side of the pond to the other. "I thought you hated the water." Lily's silence filled the air. "You threatened to kill me if I ever tried to make you swim."

She'd stopped and stood in the water. It came up to her shoulder blades there. Her eyes brushed the darkness of it and she ran a hand over her lips.

"I made a mistake."

Peter watched her silently for a moment, listening to her unspoken words.

"It's getting late." Lily didn't seem to hear as she fell back into the water once again, moving rhythmically against it.

"And Will's missing," Peter added.

"I know. He's gone back." Lily paused, her eyes searching out his, groping for them in the darkness. "Peter, did I make a mistake?"

He shook his head. "I don't know."

He waited a moment, but she was silent, so Peter turned back the way he had come and Lily returned to her lonesome swimming.

Prison

Capture

Lily moved leisurely over the forest floor, her cape whirling around her as she approached Sherwood Road. She tugged at her simple peasant's shirt, feeling unbalanced without her sword, and nervous too, but it was dangerous enough to risk Nottingham in a man's clothes. Lily dared not approach it with a large and obvious weapon like the sword.

She froze. Somewhere nearby she had heard a grating, the familiar grating of steel being drawn from a scabbard. Lily wrapped her hand around her dagger and stepped forward, her eyes darting into the darkness of the forest.

She fell forward and pain shot up her leg. Lily drew in a sharp breath, holding back any cry, and looked down at the injured limb. Sunk into the muscle by her ankle was a sharp peg, holding down a net and she would have laughed at the irony of missing the net to be speared by the peg, only the pain was too great.

The pointed wood was dark with Lily's blood

and as she bent down to it, it dug even deeper. Grunting with the effort, she pulled the stake out, gritting her teeth as splinters slipped into her muscle. She almost cried out, but contained her pain.

The net sprang back, freed from its constraints. Lily didn't move as it fell against the underbrush, rustling it, but her eyes scanned the shadows. Nothing moved. She crouched down and peeled her torn pant leg from her skin.

The flesh was torn and bloody. Lily ripped a piece of cloth from her shirt and wrapped it tightly around her leg. She froze suddenly as footsteps approached, then raced to tie the bandage.

The footsteps were almost on top of her now and when she stood up she already had her dagger out, tucked inside her cape.

He had seen her. Lily knew that, for the footsteps paused, then began to circle. She couldn't run to the cave. She couldn't run at all, for her leg ached and trembled beneath her. She had no weapon except for her dagger which was only good for close combat, and so she did the one thing left to do. She pulled her cape around her, carefully covering the male attire that she wore, and then looked around.

"Hello? Hello? Is someone there?" The footsteps stopped, then continued. "Please! Please help me!" Lily's accent had become that of a lady and it trembled with an adopted fear. "Is someone there?"

A tall dark-haired man stepped from the trees, frowning slightly. He held a sword in his hand, but his arm was relaxed, not ready to attack. Lily smiled at him.

"Thank God. I've been praying that someone would come along." She looked around, frowning. "I hurt my leg when I fell off my horse and I have no idea where I am. They say there are outlaws here, too!" She stopped. "You're not an outlaw, are you?"

He smiled, holding his sword with a practised hand. "No." And he swung.

Lily tried to duck, but the flat of the blade caught her across her chest and she doubled over in pain, gasping for air. The man laughed, circling her.

"What kind of outlaw are you, pulling a phony accent like that? Any fool could see through it."

Lily shrugged weakly. "That's why I used it for you."

He swung at her again, but she ducked, caught his arm and sliced it with her dagger. He jumped back in pain.

"At least Robin Hood taught you something!" he snorted.

"Not that again! Robin Hood has taught me nothing." Lily sneered, crouching low and eyeing the man. He only laughed.

"Then tell me where he is and I'll let you go."

"You moronic ass!" She laughed weakly, picking up a forked stick and leaning on it. "I don't know where he is! I've never met him."

"Don't play games with me!" he roared, charging at her, his sword outstretched. Lily threw the knife, but it only grazed his arm. Weaponless now, she swung the stick, catching him under his chin and then she rolled under his arm to the knife. Curling her fingers around it, she struggled to get up, but to no avail, and so Lily rolled again, onto her knees. The man was watching her and she could hear others approaching, but she only grabbed hold of a tree and pulled herself to her feet.

But then, hands clamped down on her arms, twisting them behind her. Lily growled softly, struggling enough to sink her knife into one of the Foresters. A yelp of pain went up and then they had her knife, and they tied her and gagged her and picked her up.

The man who had fought her frowned. "Is she important?"

"Aye, sir. I've seen her around. High up the criminal ladder, I'd say."

"Well, if she's important than I'll expect a good pay, you hear? Tell that to your lord sheriff!" He frowned. "Oh, never mind! I'll tell him myself."

He looked down at Lily and laughed. "Moronic ass, did you say?" He cuffed her across the side of her already spinning head.

"Move on, boys! Let's show your master your catch, shall we?" And he laughed again.

A Nottingham Welcome

The guards held Lily upside down and swung her around. Her head cracked off the wall and she cursed, feeling it throb already. She could hear the blood rushing past her ears. The guards shifted her in their arms and she almost fell to the floor.

"Make up your bloody minds!" she yelled.

"Tut, tut," a voice murmured and a pair of shiny boots stepped into her view. They were dark leather, high cut and obviously expensive. Her thief's mind priced them, then she turned her eyes upward, over the richly draped frame, past the clipped beard, pale lips and sharp nose until she rested her sights on a pair of colourless eyes that watched her with a distinct amusement in their depths; the eyes of Robert de Rainault, Sheriff of Nottingham.

"My dear," the silky voice continued, rising and falling effortlessly in a soft lilt. "Such language! Young ladies do not speak in such a manner."

"This one does."

"There," he smiled. "Not a curse! Now that wasn't

too hard, was it?"

"Go to hell!" She glared at him and then closed her lips tightly, pressing them together until all their colour faded. The sheriff continued to watch her, but his words were only to the guards.

"Who is she?"

"I've seen her before," one man said. "She seemed the leader of the troops I've seen. Good fighter. No question that she's a thief."

"Close to Hood?"

"Don't know. I can call in a spy and find out."

The sheriff waved his hand dismissively. "That's not necessary. If she knows Hood, she'll know where he is and we can kill her eventually. One more dead outlaw."

The guard shifted nervously. "Milord, the mercenary you hired wants to know how important she is. Expects a bit more money, you see."

"Well, tell him she's nothing and pay him the usual. And tell the squires to find a reward poster or prison record or anything about her. I want to know who she is."

The sheriff smiled suddenly, the well-kept moustache above his lip curling with his mouth.

"Something the matter, Milord?" the guard asked. The sheriff shook his head.

"Not at all. She's a pleasant surprise." He smiled again and his hand lifted Lily's head for a moment. She pulled away. His smile widened. "More exciting than I had expected."

He laughed suddenly and turned away. "Put her in the tower," he called over his shoulder as he ascended the throne and settled into it. "And choose the tortures carefully." He smiled at Lily's sullen face. "No visible marks. Be sure of that."

*****

Lily did not bother to fight as they carried her up the stairs, knowing that the fall would kill all of them. Flight after flight passed below and then solid stone floor, and the creaking of a door. The doorway passed over them and the guards turned her upright. Her hands and feet were tied and she balanced unsteadily, letting them support her, their hands under her arms, her elbows resting below their ears.

As the third guard stepped forward to unlock the set of chains on the wall, Lily brought her elbows up and forwards, knocking the two men onto their faces, their noses cracking off the stone floor and spraying blood across the room. Lily tore at the ropes with her teeth as the third guard whirled around and towards her. Failing there, she used her fists as a club, hitting him across the head. He stopped, stunned for a moment, and she tried again to loosen the ropes. They began to fray, but by then the other guards were on their feet again, their noses bleeding heavily. They circled her and lifted her off the ground by her bonds. One drew his hand back into a fist, but the others shook their heads.

"No marks."

"She broke my nose!"

"The sheriff will break it off if you touch her!"

The man frowned, but lowered his hand.

They held her against the wall, chaining one hand, then cutting her bonds and chaining the other one, repeating this on her feet. Lily calmed as the last shackle was secured, her body and mouth still.

The guards stepped back and surveyed her, their eyes scrutinizing. One of them wiped his nose with his arm, smearing blood up to his elbow. He snorted, then smiled suddenly, exposing brown teeth.

They howled as they stepped out the door, locking it behind them. Lily could hear their laughter as they descended the stairs, echoing throughout the tower, and she shivered. Her eyes swept the room, seeking sunlight, but it was a solid cage. She was a child of the forest and was locked away from it, without even its light to comfort her.

Nottingham Hospitality

They came for her so long afterwards that she had lost track of all time. It may have been weeks, months or only days. She hadn't counted. When she slept she saw the moon and the sun together, both brilliant, and she did not know how they had become friends. She was hungry and thirsty. They had brought her water some time ago. Was it yesterday? It had been a damp cloth that she had sucked dry and then tried to eat. So this was her torture.

She leaned her head against the wall when they came in, her eyes closed, her hearing seeming sharper than ever before. Their clothes rustled, hurting her head. She forced her eyes to open, seeing blurred forms. One reached for her.

"So, little warrior," the guard laughed. "Where's your fight now?"

He unlocked the shackle and then ducked as her fist flew at his nose. Another guard grabbed her wrist, pinning it to the wall. She stopped struggling. They tied her and lifted her up and carried her away. The ropes cut into her skin, but she didn't care. She curled up, trying to block the sounds that tore at her ears, but hearing them just the same.

They sat her in a chair in what seemed to be a hallway and proceeded to pour wine down her throat. It was sweet and sticky and wonderful. She gulped it greedily and then was sick on the floor.

Her head was pounding, but she felt refreshed and somehow relieved. They pulled her to her feet, forcing her down the hall, but now she walked, her chin held proudly although her stomach still churned and the air seemed heavy against her mind.

Then they pushed her inside a room and moved away from her. She forced her eyes to focus and they scanned the room, moving slowly over the rich tapestries and rugs until they came to rest on the bed.

"No," Lily said, her voice harsh in her dry throat. "There is no way . . ."

Footsteps assaulted her ears and she turned toward them, seeing the gleaming form of the sheriff, his smile still the same as at their last meeting.

"I'm glad to see that you still have some fight left in you," he greeted her. She felt sick again.

He gripped her wrist tightly, too tightly. It hurt her, his nails digging into her skin. And then he forced her to face him, gripping her by the hair, her face inches from his. Defiant, she spit in his face, her anger shaking off the sluggishness from her limbs.

"You little witch!" he snarled violently, but she brought her knee up into his groin and he crumpled. The guards rushed forward as she leapt on him, her fists delivering sharp blows, his nose crumpling beneath her knuckles.

Then she felt hands on her arms, pulling her away, swinging her around, and the fists turned on her. Then the sheriff's voice rose above it all, shrieking now, gurgling over the blood running down his face.

"Don't kill her yet!" he screamed as the room spun around and her blood began to stain the floor. "She knows where Robin Hood is! But so help me God, I want her to be hurting. I want her to experience more pain than anyone ever has before her!"

As she fell to the floor, Lily had no doubt that she would do just that.

Robin

Family

Robin crouched low, ducking below a branch that stretched across his path. He could hear Little John behind him, but kept going, watching as the towers of the castle came into view.

"I don't think we lost them," John said quietly. "Where are we, anyway?"

"Behind Nottingham Castle." Robin laughed quietly as John groaned.

"Just keep walking," Robin said. "Carry some wood." He was already piling sticks into his own arms. John frowned.

"It's not winter. Why would we have firewood?"

"Some people think ahead. Come on."

Robin pulled his tattered peasant's cloak around himself and staggered from the small woods, out into the light and the open field that surrounded the castle. He didn't bother looking at the building. He knew it by heart. Four tall walls, joined at three corners by round towers and at one corner by the L-shaped building where the sheriff lived. To Robin's left stood the gate tower, stuck in the middle of one wall. Robin kept his eyes on the ground, even as his mind fought with his urge to see if he could sneak inside this place again.

"Robin." John whispered, stopping.

"Come on, John!" Robin said, turning back to glance at his friend.

The big man only stared upward. "Dear God!"

Robin followed his gaze to the top of the nearest tower. On its roof stood three men. They held a struggling form on the lip of the tower, pushing her head downwards, toward the ground that lay far below. She fought them, or tried to, wriggling and kicking.

Robin could hear the soldiers shouting, but could not make out the words. They seemed to be questioning her, but that was pointless as they were pushing down on her chin, making it impossible for her to even open her mouth, much less speak. She slipped a little farther out from the lip of the tower and Robin could hear John begin to pray. Robin murmured some Hail Marys, but kept his eyes on the girl, trying to figure out some way to save her, but nothing came to mind.

And then, one of the soldiers crumpled from sight. The girl pulled away, out onto the lip of the tower, but the two remaining soldiers were closing in. She seemed to be wounded, for she swayed and clutched at her side, but then she turned and leapt.

Robin leapt back as she hit the ground, barely a meter from him. The soldiers on the tower shouted and turned, running down the stairs and out of sight.

The girl pulled herself onto her stomach, then up onto her elbow. She glared at the two outlaws and they dared not move.

"Get . . . away." Her words were filled with effort and, as she tried to get to her knees, her eyes rolled back in her head and she fell to the ground. She did not move.

Robin bent over the crumpled body and slid his arms under her. She was as light as a rag doll and her limbs hung as limply as one. Her head rolled back and a silver locket glinted against her pale skin, clinging to the sweat that had gathered in the curve of her collar bone. The engraving was clogged with dirt, but that only made the letters darker. They read: LILY. Robin almost dropped her.

His fingers itched to touch the locket, to feel it in his hand again, but he didn't move. He stared at the battered, bloody face of the young woman he held and it was the face of the child he had known, now bruised and broken.

"We need a horse!" he called to John, even as he heard the gates opening and the approaching soldiers.

"Heck! We need two horses," John snapped sarcastically.

"Well go get them!" Robin adjusted Lily in his arms so that her head rested against his chest. John frowned at his friend, but he carefully selected a heavy stick from his pile of kindling.

Three soldiers raced around the corner, each on a horse. John swung his stick. One soldier tumbled off and Robin grabbed the horse's reins. He slid Lily into the saddle and jumped on behind her before she had time to fall off.

"Let's go!" he called to John, urging the horse ahead. Behind him sounded another thud and John had a horse. The two outlaws turned to the third rider, but he only paled and raced back to the safety of Nottingham Castle's stone walls.

John kicked his horse toward the road that led to Sherwood. Robin let his own horse follow, not bothering to lead. Lily moaned softly, seeming amazingly fragile in his arms. He remembered her funeral, then shook it off. He refused to be afraid.

Dreaming

Robin clutched the sides of the wagon as it tipped, but he couldn't hold onto it. He felt himself flying through the air and into the water. Cold. The water swallowed him into a world of silence and he couldn't breathe and there was nothing.

But then he was on the surface again and the water roared by his ears, pounding and racing, and a hand reached out of the water, groping toward him, trying to grab hold of anything. It was a child's hand and a child's face accompanied it, appearing suddenly beside him, crying and screaming, begging him to help. He tried, stretching out his hands toward the girl, calling, but the current swept her along and she disappeared beneath the water, crying for him. He plunged through the water, still reaching for her.

"LILY!!"

*****

Robin sat up as his scream rang through the

house. He fell out of his chair and scrambled across the floor toward the bedroom.

The door opened easily and he was able to enter without a sound. Marian stared at him in alarm from her post beside the bed, then realized his screams had announced no real danger. She frowned, but said nothing. Robin did not even notice Marian, only moved closer to the bed.

Lily lay still against the white sheets as she had done for so long now. Robin put a hand to her forehead, but she wasn't hot. Her face was calm, her fingers still. Her breathing seemed less forced than before.

Robin stepped away from her, smiling sheepishly at Marian. He turned, edging out the door and into his chair. His eyelids seemed to be made of lead. They sank again and again, but he fought sleep, not wanting to return to his dreams. Soon, however, the battle was lost. Sleep reigned and Robin returned to his dreams and to the past.

Awakenings

Marian moved carefully through the bedroom without making a sound. Will Scarlett sat in the chair beside the bed, asleep. His breathing made a soft whistling sound that floated through the room. Marian smiled, then turned to Lily.

The girl lay curled up, one hand resting on the edge of the splints encasing her lower right leg. Marian gently lifted this hand and laid it on the blankets. Lily moved in her sleep at this intrusion and Marian stopped, waiting. When no more movement was forthcoming, she turned and left the room.

Marian moved past Robin in the next room. He also sat sleeping. She paused, kissed her husband softly and moved toward the table, setting it carefully with wooden bowls and spoons. She heard Robin stir.

"Don't bother getting up," she said over her shoulder, carefully straightening the flowers she'd set in the middle of the table. "I just checked on Lily."

His voice was sleepy. "Any change?"

"She looks like she's sleeping."

Robin sighed. "No change." Marian turned and he smiled at her wearily. "I'm sorry to bring you into all of this, Marian, as though this thief's life isn't enough! You must think I'm a fool."

Marian shook her head, causing the blond hair that was not tucked under her cap to sway about her face. "I don't think that."

"I know those looks you're always giving me," Robin said. "How do I even know it's her?"

Marian began smoothing out the tattered cloth that covered the makeshift table. "Will said her name is Lily."

"It's not enough for you, though, is it?"

Marian came over to where he sat. "It doesn't matter, Robin. You need this."

She moved to kiss him, but they both froze as a noise came from the bedroom, a whisper. It was a female voice. Robin jumped up and to the door.

Lily sat in the bed, Will across from her. Will's face was complete disbelief, but he was somehow managing to convince Lily of their safety. Lily looked up.

"Robin."

"Lily?" He had so many things to say to her, but none of them came out of his mouth. "Are you all right?"

She nodded. "Where's Peter?"

"Who?"

She turned to Will then, her eyes wide, her fingers touching the splints on her leg. "Will, where's Peter? I need to see him."

"He's not here."

Lily frowned, then nodded. "Of course he's not here." She looked up. "Robin?"

"How do you know my name?"

She frowned. "I just know you."

Will opened his mouth to say something, but Lily broke in. "Robin, I need to go home."

He shook his head. "You just woke up! You've been out for a week!"

"But none of my men knows where I am! What if they try to break into the prison?"

"Lily, you can go home soon, but not now. You're hurt."

"This?" She gestured at her leg. "This isn't bad!"

"You're staying here!"

Marian frowned at Robin, then turned to Lily, who gazed at her without recognition. "Lily, you've been out cold for a week."

Will frowned. "Maybe I can go?"

Lily shook her head. "We never showed you the way." She was looking tired and pale again. Marian glared at Will and Robin, then turned back to Lily.

"The only solution is for you to get better. I'll

get you something to eat and these fellows will let you rest." She nodded at Robin before leaving the room. "No arguments."

Robin barely noticed Marian's warning. He only stared at Lily. "I can't believe you're here."

Lily shrugged and smiled and glanced away. "Well, I am."

Robin nodded. "It's good to see your eyes." He turned to go, but behind him he could hear Lily, her voice pleading.

"Will, tell him. I need to see Peter."

Progress

A few days later, Robin was outside, walking slowly along the path that led through the camp. He stopped, waiting as Lily caught up with him. She swung her crutches before her, moving along unsteadily, a grin on her face.

"See, Robin. I can do it."

"With crutches," he reminded her.

"Not for long."

He had walked too fast and was already ahead of Lily. While waiting, he watched her some more. The splints were less noticeable now that she was on her feet, but they still held her leg unnaturally straight.

"Does it hurt?" he asked Lily. She shook her head.

"No." She shifted the crutches under her arms. "Well, these hurt a little."

"Don't blame me. Marian got them."

"Tell her they're worth it." Lily smiled. "I like her, Robin. She's sweet. You've been married what, two days?"

"Two years," he corrected her mocking voice. She snorted.

"I'm impressed."

There was silence then, until Robin managed to choke out a question he'd been thinking for while.

"And you and this Peter?"

"Hardly the same thing. Friends for ten years. His daughter's named after me." Robin wasn't sure if she put that piece of information in to show their friendship or Peter's marriage.

"What is he going to say about your leg?" he asked.

"He'll shake his head and sigh at me. That's all. He's used to me arriving home in bandages."

"Hit him with your crutches, then," Robin laughed. "You don't have to take that from him."

Lily grinned. "I'll do that when I see him." She stopped. "When will I see him, Robin?"

"Soon."

She grinned, then focused on her crutches once again.

Coming Home

It was only two days later that saw Lily and Robin walking down Sherwood Road, eyeing the bushes carefully. Lily moved along quickly on her crutches, keeping up to Robin easily. He stopped, but she kept on past him. He called after her.

"Lily, I don't see anyone."

"We just have to walk a little longer."

Robin frowned. "Can you? We didn't bring a horse."

"We couldn't have brought one," she said. "We don't have room in the stable for another two horses."

"At least you could have used one," Robin said, but Lily shook her head.

"Why do you think that I need a horse? You're the one who's complaining."

"Lily, I don't see anyone. Maybe your men went off somewhere to do something else. There's more to this than just robbing travelers, you know."

She shook her head. "They're here, somewhere along this stretch! This is where we always come!"

She stopped, then grinned, pointing ahead. "There!"

Lily moved ahead on her crutches, outdistancing the others, moving toward what seemed to be an empty stretch of road. She shouted loudly.

"Peter! Peter! It's me!"

There was a rustling in the trees and bushes that lined the road and a large blond man stepped out, staring at Lily. Her face broke into the widest grin Robin had ever seen, but Peter could only stare.

"PETER!!!"

"Lily!" He ran to her and pulled her against his chest, enveloping her, crutches and all. "Lily. Thank you, God."

The last was almost a whisper. Robin only heard it as he reached them. Lily disentangled herself from Peter and rested her weight on her crutches.

"Jumped off a tower," she shrugged as Peter looked at the crutches.

Robin nodded. "She had splints on it and she was out for a week before that."

Lily grinned wider than ever. "Peter, this is my brother Robin."

Robin shook the offered hand, waiting to be bombarded with questions, but none came. Peter only nodded.

Behind him, more men began to gather, creeping out of the woods. One of them ran to Lily.

"Lily, are you all right?"

"I'm fine, Tristan."

"We thought you were dead."

She shrugged. "Well, I'm not."

The others just stood around, staring at Robin until Lily glared at them. "Is that hospitality? Robin is my brother, so everyone be nice and show a little friendliness."

She moved ahead of them on her crutches toward the wood. Peter walked beside Robin.

"So you're Peter," Robin said.

Peter nodded. "And you're you."

*****

Robin waved away the offered food. His stomach was already stuffed. He felt warm and contented, even when he looked around the fire and saw the mixture of friendliness and suspicion that showed on the faces the firelight drew from the darkness.

"So, Lily. This is your big brother, is it?" a voice called. "What's his name?"

"Robin," she said from her seat in the roots of the nearest tree.

"So he really is Robin Hood?"

She nodded and the men laughed loudly. "Yeah. Ha ha," she said, but with a smile on her face. Robin frowned.

"Why are they laughing?"

She smiled. "I've never liked you very much."

Robin nodded, wondering why, but then another voice called out.

"So what stories of great adventure can you tell us to thrill our dull lives?" The request was friendly and Robin smiled.

"I'll tell you about the time we took the sheriff to a dinner of the King's deer in our own camp, and then charged him 300 gold pieces for it! Then we tied him to his horse backwards and sent him home with his face in the beast's tail!"

"We've all heard that one before."

Robin nodded. "Then, the one about the tinker who was sent to serve me a warrant. I stole the warrant and . . ."

"We've heard it all before."

"Then, why doesn't Lily tell us how she broke her leg?" Robin suggested.

Lily glanced around the campfire and shrugged. "I jumped off a tower."

Tristan stared at her. "Why?"

"To get off it."

Laughter and shouts. "Did you ever think of using the stairs?"

Lily laughed. "And take the easy way out? You know me better than that!"

Even Robin laughed at that. The conversation turned to other adventures and other people. Lily had succeeded in getting the attention off her injury.

No one spoke of it throughout the rest of the night.

As people finally began to slip away and the fire had burnt to embers, Lily made her way over to Robin. She leaned on her crutches and smiled wearily.

"Come on inside. I'll find a bed for you."

Tristan appeared behind her. "You're tired, Lily and the cave's in chaos. I'll find a place for him."

Surprisingly, Lily nodded and turned toward the cave. Robin did so too and Tristan showed him to a small bedroom.

"I hope this is a good room for you. We're kind of crowded." The boy stood in the doorway a moment, shifting his weight from foot to foot. Robin glanced at him.

"Is there something you want to know?" he asked. The boy frowned.

"Well, only – how did you lose Lily?"

Robin winced, but nodded. "We were traveling and the wagon tipped. My entire family was thrown into the water. My mother drowned and Lily was washed away." He rubbed his eyes. "We never found her."

The next time Robin looked up, Tristan was gone. Robin sighed and slid under the blankets that were piled high on the bed. He closed his eyes and, for once, the past did not seep into his dreams. He slept.

Good-byes

Peter watched Lily from an upstairs window in the cave. She was dancing below him, her sword drawn and jabbing at Robin. Peter was happy just to watch her. She was laughing, shouting joking insults at her brother while avoiding his blows skillfully. She looked small next to Robin, but never vulnerable, never weak, only strong and proud and contented. Peter could not remember a time when she'd looked as happy as she did now.

Anna pulled on Peter's arm, annoyed at her father's lack of attention. "Daddy, what are you looking at?"

"Lily. Come on up and see her."

Anna stood on tiptoe to see out the window. "Who is that with her?"

"Her brother Robin." Peter turned away from the window and picked up little Lily from the bed. The baby blew bubbles at him and shrieked giddily. Peter held her above his head and she screamed with laughter, spraying spittle around her. Peter laughed softly.

"Anna?"

The little girl looked up from under her yellow hair. "Yes, da?"

"Let's go see Lily."

*****

Lily looked up at the sound of her name and saw Anna running across the field to her. Robin turned too and Lily touched his chest with her sword.

"You're dead."

"The fight was over!"

"I don't remember saying that."

Robin smiled in defeat and put his sword away just as Anna reached them. She stopped suddenly, stared at Robin and laughed.

"I know you! I saw your picture in the village."

"And what is your name, Milady?" Robin asked, bowing and kissing her hands. Anna grinned and curtsied clumsily.

"Anna Margaret Semmons, Milord."

"I'm delighted to meet you." Robin kept his upper-class accent pronounced until she squealed with laughter.

"Do they really talk like that?"

"They do," Lily broke in. Robin glanced up at her as Peter reached them. The older man nodded at Robin.

"Your horse is ready. She's a lovely little mare. Lily picked her out for you."

Lily frowned, then turned to Robin. "I guess it's time for you to go home, Rob."

No one spoke for a moment and she smiled. "Don't worry. This isn't the end. How big can Sherwood be? We'll see each other again." She laughed. "Come on. We'll go get your horse."

They turned into the stables. In the center of the aisle stood a dun-coloured mare. It already wore a saddle and bridle. Lily smiled and the horse snorted loudly.

"How do you like her?" she asked.

"She's lovely."

"She's yours." Lily shrugged. "Call it a good-bye present."

"Thanks."

"Well, it's not as if she's mine!" Lily laughed. "A certain baron will want your hide if he sees you on this horse!"

Robin grinned and Lily ducked her head, digging in around her belt. "I had these made for you." She handed him two leather-bound parcels. "One's for you, the other for Will."

Robin had already unwrapped one. A hunting horn lay in his hand, made out of a wild boar's tusk.

"They sound like no others," Lily said quietly. "Three sharp notes, and we're on our way."

"You worry too much."

Her smile was sombre. "Three sharp notes. Remember."

"Fine, then," he laughed. "I'll remember. What if you need my help?"

"I don't think so." She raised a skeptical eyebrow.

"And why not?"

"They call you the ghosts of Sherwood at times, because you, like ghosts, are rarely seen." She smiled. "We are the real ghosts. No one even knows we're here."

"Point taken." Robin leapt into the saddle. "Thank you."

She smiled. "There is one other thing I want you to take," she said. Lily shifted her weight and pulled the crutches from underneath her arms. She swayed, then forced herself steady. She lashed the wood together and passed them up to Robin.

"Return them to Marian. I don't plan to need them anymore."

Robin nodded. As the door closed behind him and he stood alone in all of Sherwood's mystery, he raised the horn to his lips. One long, low note sounded and echoed throughout the forest. Then Robin turned the horse's head toward home.

Next Spring

Will relaxed in the saddle, the movement of the horse a gentle rhythm, welcome after the long winter inside the dark cottages of the Merry Men. Winter was a time when few travelers passed by and so the thieves waited inside for a bit of warmth, only venturing forth to distribute their hoarded goods.

Now it was spring. Will breathed it in happily. The hunting horn by his side bumped against him in the same rhythm as the horse. He reached down and held onto it, running his fingers along the smooth boar's tusk, still puzzled by its purpose, for Robin had explained none of it when he had given the horn to Will the autumn past.

Shaking off his dreaminess, Will turned around in the saddle, his eyes glancing over the scouting party behind him, then turning around again, trying to stay alert. They were all out of practice, he mused. We've grown lazy over the winter.

A twig snapped nearby, and Will's head jerked

up, instinctively leaping into the familiar wariness. Every outlaw stilled, listening.

An arrow just grazed Will's head, stinging, but nothing more. "Turn the horses!" he cried. "Run for it!"

He could see the Foresters now, on all sides, their faces gleeful. "Get off the horses! You're easy targets!" he called. "Make them your walls!"

They were sadly outnumbered. Will had brought only four other men with him. That was all. There had to be at least thirteen Foresters.

Three sharp notes. Will ripped the horn from his belt and the notes reached the clouds. He paused, waiting for the help Robin had promised. Nothing.

"Great plan, Rob," he muttered, nocking an arrow to his bow. The Foresters were bad targets, always moving, and their dark clothes blended with Sherwood's shady undergrowth. The outlaws shot anyway.

Several horses were injured by now, but none of the woodsmen had more than skin wounds. However, even without the Foresters they'd killed off, they were fighting a losing battle, running out of space, energy, and arrows.

A horn sounded nearby, long and low. Then suddenly a troop of horsemen leapt through the underbrush, swords flashing. The horses' hooves pounded the ground and their eyes were wild. The

Foresters gaped and reached for more arrows, then reconsidered as the lead rider bore down on them, riding low, sword at neck height. She smiled chillingly.

She laughed, eyes wild, catching one Forester beneath her horse's hooves. The man rolled out from underneath it and limped away, faster than he could usually walk. The Foresters ran, stumbling over one another in an effort to escape the demons they'd awakened in Sherwood's haunted depths.

Lily laughed again, and whirled Starline around, calling to her friends.

"Check for injured. Only horses? Get them patched up. You, take half home. It's crowded here. You, keep an eye out for a return party. Isn't it great, boys?"

Will saw her eyes alight on him and she burst into a surprised grin. She leapt down and into his arms.

"I've missed you," she said, pulling away. She frowned. "You're bleeding."

"You're beautiful." She laughed again, her cheeks flushed with excitement, her eyes dancing, and Will smiled. The Foresters were wrong. They had awakened no spirit, for no woodland nymph could possibly have been so beautiful to him.

The Story

"Repeat that please, Captain."

The voice was chillingly cold, composed and deadly, stopping the captain's hysterical testimony. Until now, the sheriff had sat in the throne he had erected, silently listening, his chin resting in one hand, the fingers laced around one eye. The captain fingered his mud-splattered cap and bit his lip.

"We almost had them and then a demon . . ."

"Are you feeling well, Captain?"

"Yes, sir."

"Then why are you telling me wives' tales?" Robert de Rainault bellowed, hands clenching the armrests of his chair, face white with rage. "There are no ghosts, dragons, elves, demons, or any other such nonsense in Sherwood Forest! There is only a measly pack of scrawny thieves!"

"This was a woman!"

The sheriff looked up, then snapped his fingers at his scribe. "Didn't we have a woman in the tower? The one who escaped?" The scribe nodded.

"There. You see?" he sneered at the captain.

"She wasn't with them. Scarlett called on a horn, and this . . . figure appeared," the captain stammered, wiping his brow. "She was on a black monster of a horse, that breathed fire and had red eyes, and she was elfin, with ice-cold eyes and voice, carrying a sword made of bone! Behind her were men with dead eyes and they were obeying her, as though they had no will of their own!"

"Of course, Captain," the sheriff sighed. "She's a nymph who captures men's souls and makes them her slaves. It all makes sense to me now." He was about to reach for a long rope that hung beside him when the man cried out.

"I can find her!"

The sheriff paused, his hand on the rope, raising one expertly plucked brow. "Oh?"

"I got a good look at her face."

"Please, go on."

"Maybe you were right. Maybe she is human, and if she is, I'm the only one who got a good look. She was always moving, so no one else saw."

The sheriff brought down his manicured hand and laid it in his lap. "Dark hair, round face, dark fiery eyes?"

"Yes. How . . .?"

"I remember beautiful women." He smiled cruelly, revealing sharp, pointed teeth. "Of course she was beaten so badly, the face I saw was a bit

. . . distorted." He laughed, and the captain and the guards and the scribe all joined in obediently.

"All right, Captain, find her. Why not? If you find her, I get to invite a charming young lady back into my household, and if not . . ." He eyed the rope. "The bell will toll." He smiled again.

Three Months Later

A small huddle of outlaws made their way towards Sherwood Road. They were seven. Three were new to the life of the Merry Men so their first expedition was simple: accompany one of the parties sent thieving. It was a basic job, but like all their work, fraught with peril.

The men had no time to even yell when large hands were clamped over their mouths and they were pulled into the underbrush.

"We don't want you," the voice of Guy of Gisbourne hissed in their ears. "You're just bait." Ropes were secured, but one of the outlaws stepped away, smiling.

"Guy, my good man!" he grinned. Gisbourne frowned at him.

"Where's the horn?"

"I have it!" he snapped as two of the Foresters approached threateningly. "But don't I get a reward or something? You try living in the woods for a month!"

"Listen, soldier!" Gisbourne snarled. "These

slobs have made you too cocky. You'll follow orders with no backtalk! Now give me the horn!"

The man glared at him but obeyed, stepping into line with the Foresters and drawing his sword. The remaining outlaws watched him with hate in their eyes as the notes rang out into the air.

Help did appear, but slowly and cautiously. The lead rider, they all knew, although mainly from stories. Both captors and captives grew silent as they watched her. Slowly, looking puzzled, she walked her horse in a circle. Something caught her eye and she wheeled the beast around.

"It's a trap," she screamed, but already the forest rang with swords clashing. "Get out!" Her stallion plunged into the fray as she beat down the Foresters trying to grasp the greatest prize, her.

"Lily! Get out!" a voice cried, as those still able to ran for safety.

"But . . ." she turned finally, avoiding looking at the struggles of her comrades as ropes tightened around their wrists. Her eyes met Peter's for a moment and her face fell as he was pulled away. She turned tortured eyes to someone else she knew, and rage filled them.

"Gisbourne!" she roared, as she turned her horse away. "I will kill you. I swear it!"

Guy of Gisbourne said nothing as she kicked her heels into Starline and galloped away. He only turned to leave, taking his prisoners with him.

Damage Control

In the cramped quarters of Robin's hut they held a meeting. Will, Much, John, Robin, Lily and two others of the Merry Men were there. The six men sat at the table, one candle between them, while Lily paced in the shadows.

"How could they have gotten the horn?" Robin asked.

"You and Will have the only two," Much reminded him. "Check."

"Mine's missing," Will said. "I found out after they left. I was going to rail at whoever it was when the party returned."

"How could a spy get in among us?" John sighed. "Are you sure he was with the Foresters?" They all looked at Lily who was rubbing her forehead as though it ached. She didn't look up.

"Yes."

"Well, what now?"

"What do you mean, what now?" Lily snapped. "We go in and get them out!"

The man stared at her. "You can't expect to

break in there?"

"I've done it before."

Will nodded to show that it was true.

"How will we do it?"

She shrugged. "Get in, start a fight, pick the locks, and hope to God that we get out alive."

The man smirked and turned back to the table, rolling his eyes at John, who only glared at him.

"My men were taken too, Lily," Robin said softly.

"They are not just my men! They are my family! They trusted me, and I let them be taken away! I am not going to let them down again!" Lily's voice fell. "You haven't been there, Robin. You don't know what it's like. The sheriff wanted to keep me and Will alive. That's the only reason we survived. I don't know what he plans to do with them."

"You want us to help?" The same man shrugged. "I don't see why we'd risk it."

"Now, wait just a minute!" Will leapt to his feet. "Have you forgotten so quickly all that she's done for us?"

"For her own gain."

Robin growled softly, but did not move, did not get in Lily's way. The other three, who knew Lily, not just her reputation, grew silent. They watched Lily carefully as she laid her hands on the table, and glared at the man who had spoken.

"I'll tell you why you'll risk it. My fellows got

caught cleaning up after you, or have you forgotten how we've spent so much time rescuing your carcasses?" She stood up. "I'm not going to grovel for help. This is not repayment. The horn was a gift. I just thought that it would be a nice gesture for you to show Robin some gratitude by keeping his sister alive!"

The man glanced at Robin, who said nothing, only raised an eyebrow. "You are alive."

"Yes, but if I don't get help from you, I'll get the four men left at home, and die trying to free the rest."

"We'll be there." Robin's voice was the still one he used when he could not be moved from a decision. Lily smiled at him, her eyes weary.

The man who had spoken against Lily grunted. "The men must be volunteers."

Robin did not seem to have heard. "We'll be there, Lil."

She nodded, suddenly looking very old, very tired. "I hope so."

The Beginning of the End

At the gates to the courtyard a thin, pale man stood, his eyes sunken and white, his beard unkempt. He stopped each person who passed by, desperately searching their faces and vehicles. The little dignity he still held was in the tattered soldier uniform that he wore, the arms still proclaiming his rank as captain.

"What are you rooting around in my cart for?" one passerby grunted, reining in his nervous, muddied horse.

"A woman," the captain muttered. The other man snorted and the captain cringed at the derision. "She's an outlaw."

"If you ask me, son," the driver of the cart chuckled, "You'd better spread out your search. She'd have to be pretty stupid to walk right into the sheriff's front yard!"

The captain waved him by grudgingly and the cart rode through the gate, then turned, ducking in behind one of the buildings. The driver leapt down, opened a hatch and Lily tumbled out, Giant right behind her. She reached back into the compartment and pulled out two swords, tossing one to the driver with a grin.

"Well, here we are, Dickon," she greeted him. "Right in the sheriff's front yard." She smiled sadly as she got to her feet and he turned away. "If I don't see you again . . ." She shook her head, attempted a half-hearted grin and let him go. He disappeared and Lily turned to unharnessing Starline from the wagon and wiping the mud off him.

"Hush, boy. It's just market day," she soothed as his ears went up. Even here, the noises and smells were overwhelming; the swarms of people and goods created something overpowering for every sense.

"Stay here," Lily ordered, then quietly slipped away, her cape swirling around her.

She had forgotten how much she hated it in town. There were too many people too close to her, all reeking and grabbing and pushing. The merchants reached out, trying to attract her attention, but she had no wish to see them. Her eyes searched desperately for a familiar face. Someone grabbed her wrist and she felt herself being dragged into one of the alleyways between the buildings.

She whirled around, her hand on her knife and there stood a man. One eye was covered by a patch, the other was half-closed, but the eye behind the lid moved rapidly to every corner. He wore a long gray cape, the edges frayed and the entire thing covered in grime. His head was wrapped in a bloody bandage and Lily grinned.

"Will!" she laughed, embracing him. "You never looked so good!"

He smiled and opened his free eye. "You should see Robin."

"Is he here? Of course he's here!" She stopped. "Is anyone else here? I mean, it's great to see you and I know that you would come alone and that is great. I'm really thankful, but . . ."

". . .there's safety in numbers?"

She shook her head. "I just want to win today. I have to win today."

He grinned. "We're all here."

"All?" Her eyes grew wide and he could tell that she was suppressing the urge to jump about in delight, to cast her eyes over the crowd and see those familiar faces.

"Well, not the elderly, or the women and children, or the sick, but everyone who is healthy and able is here." He beamed down at her. "They all wanted to come."

"Oh, Will!" She jumped on him, kissing him in sheer delight. "Where's Robin?"

"What?" he muttered underneath her mouth.

She repeated her question and he blinked. "Oh, um . . . in the stable, I think, or around it. We're sort of milling around."

She nodded and turned to leave, then stopped. Her face grew solemn. "Will, if I don't survive today, take care of Starline, will you?"

"Lily, you're going to make it. We're going to be fine."

"I don't know. I feel death nearby." She forced a smile, kissed him lightly and leapt back into the milling crowd, struggling against it to reach the stables.

The people pushed past her, bustling and shouting and clutching packages to themselves. Lily pushed out of the flow and leaned against the stable wall in relief. She closed her eyes, but the noise and the smell of the people still assaulted her senses. She retreated from it all, inside the dark stable.

It was impeccably clean and smelled of leather and horses. A small door was directly ahead of her, but she ignored it, assuming it led to the tack room. To her left was a long row of standing stalls, but half of them were empty. The horses lifted their heads, wary, making no sound. Their coats gleamed in the dim light and their halters were studded with glinting brass. In front of one of the animals stood a man, gently talking to the animal. He turned and Lily gasped.

"Robin! Your nose!"

He grinned and then winced, putting his hand over the offending appendage. He wore a long brown cape, covered in blood and manure and dust, plus a pair of crutches that rested neatly under his arms. His hands were bandaged, his hair was short and had a reddish tinge to it, and his nose . . .

"Will broke it for me." Robin shrugged. "It was part of the disguise."

"It worked! I mean, he warned me . . . but this!" Lily started to laugh, putting her hands over her mouth to try to stop the sound. She bit down on her knuckles, then finally gave up, gasping through her glee. "I never expected this." She tried to sober up, then looked at him and broke down again. "You look . . . so awful!"

"Oh, shut up," he shot back, but there was laughter in his voice. "You're one to talk. That proper peasant's cape makes you look almost a lady! I do hope your normal clothes are under that cape."

"Yes, but it fools the crowds." She lowered her voice. "They're looking for me."

"I know. They stopped us too. You get used to it." He stopped. "Are you scared?"

"No!" she laughed, too loudly. "No! A little. It's not the fight. It's the people . . . my people, I mean."

"They'll be fine."

"There's a lot of kids here, Rob. Do me a

favour and convince them to go home."

"They'll go into one of the buildings when the fighting starts anyway."

Lily nodded. "Well, then that's taken care of." She looked up, shrugged and forced a smile to her face. "I don't have a plan, you know. One of the men broke his leg and couldn't come. We're spread all over."

"That's fine. The main idea is to fight and we're organized."

"Organized!" Lily snorted. As Robin started out the door, she spoke up. "I'm glad you came." He turned and she smiled sadly. "Maybe I will get out of here alive!"

Peter's Rescue

Guy of Gisbourne looked painfully nervous on the platform beside Peter, although Peter was the one with the noose around his neck. Being cousin to the sheriff was all that had kept Gisbourne alive after he had let the outlaw girl get away. Now, any error would send an arrow through him, from the sheriff, or from her. He glanced up at the castle fearfully.

Lily already had the arrow nocked to her bow under her cloak and was sizing up her target.

"They're scared," she whispered to Robin. "Only one at a time is going to be killed. They think that any rescue will go for the gallows. This way they only lose one."

Robin eyed Peter fearfully. The big man looked off into the distance while the crowd jeered and the noose was fixed in size. The crowd laughed, only knowing that he was a thief and a murderer, and not caring either way. He had failed them by being caught. Robin turned as Lily moved.

"Don't die now!" he whispered. "We'll attack soon."

Lily whirled around and the fear in her eyes scared him. "Don't let them kill him," she whispered. "If I die, promise you'll get him out."

Robin nodded and Lily turned away quickly, still looking for a bare patch in Gisbourne's armour. He moved his hands, curling his fingers around the lever that would open the trap door below Peter's feet. An arrow soared through the air, hitting its mark with deadly accuracy. Gisbourne crumpled slowly, released from the worry of who would kill him. Lily had kept her promise.

When the outlaws saw Guy of Gisbourne die, they leapt forward in a powerful wave, roaring. The sound exploded from all directions and the peasants scattered, diving into buildings and under stalls. The outlaws clamored to reach the gallows, while the Foresters fought to keep them off. Neither approached the lone prisoner standing there, the rope still around his neck.

"This is pointless," Robin called to Lily. "We need more men."

She was already slipping through the crowd, her sword at the ready, cutting her way to the dungeons. The guards had gone to join the fray and Lily bent to the lock, her fingers carefully picking it, her ears shutting out the battle raging around her, until that beautiful click sounded.

She threw open the door and began the slow descent. The stairs echoed her footsteps and the scratching of rats. She winced at the smell from below, a reminder of her own days in the tower. Holding her breath, Lily plunged into the prison below.

The men slouched in their chains, eyeing her with a mixture of awe and disbelief. Slowly, smiles began to creep across their faces.

“Come on, guys,” she muttered, bending to pick the locks, her practised fingers doing it in seconds. Charles rubbed his wrists in relief, then stood up and followed her, his less practiced fingers imitating her work.

“This is not what I planned,” she muttered. “This wasn’t supposed to happen. How are you doing? Good. How did this whole mess happen, anyway? Me and my stupid protectiveness. He’s Robin Hood! He could have taken care of himself.”

The sentences had no pauses between them, no way to tell when she was speaking to another and when to herself, but the men just followed, chattering amongst themselves in glee. Those who knew how assisted Lily. As the last chain fell, a voice called out.

“So, is there a fight out there?”

Lily looked up, her eyes dancing, a delighted smile on her face. “Like you’ve never seen!”

A roar went up from them, her enthusiasm coursing through them like a magic elixir, restoring life to all their tired limbs They leapt up the steps and out onto the battlefield.

The Foresters gaped at the wave of woodsmen who suddenly joined their comrades, pulling arrows out of dead bodies and swords from stiff hands. The battle stretched quickly all over the courtyard and the Foresters were soon sorely wanting for fighters. The girl-demon from Sherwood swept by on her horse three times and each time the Foresters' numbers rapidly decreased.

Lily preferred being on horseback, but here it meant being an easy target, and so she finally gave up the saddle and darted in and out of the crowd, still trying to make it to the gallows. People moved aside as she raced past, her sword ready. This time, she reached the platform fairly easily and raced up the steps to Peter. He grinned as the ropes fell from his hands and throat.

"Scared?" Lily asked, grinning as he clasped her to him.

"You're right about that," he said, and swung her around, laughing.

Peter's painful gasp shook Lily, and she pulled away. She knew that sound, felt it echoing in her head, mixed with the memories of a thousand battles and a thousand deaths. They both looked numbly at the point of an arrowhead protruding from his chest.

"Oh, Peter," she whispered as he fell. "We almost made it."

He smiled weakly as death rippled over him.

"You tried." Then his hand gripped her shoulder hard. "Watch Molly. They'll go after her now that I'm dead."

"Peter, you can't die." Lily's eyes watered as she brushed the hair from his eyes. They were glazing over. "I can't do this without you! I don't know how! Peter! Look at me! Please! PETER!!!"

He was dead. Lily knew it already. She had seen it too many times before. His own blood streaked the fingers with which she closed his staring eyes. Lily lifted her old friend's hands and folded them over his chest, carefully covering his death wound with the work-roughened fingers. He could have been asleep, now that the wound was covered. Lily closed her eyes, and breathed deeply, her breath shuddering as it entered her body. The battle faded away. There was no sound, no smell, nothing. When she finally opened her eyes, there was nothing but the door to Nottingham castle. She silently picked up her sword from where she'd dropped it and stepped forward, her eyes still on the door, her mind on the man who lay behind it.

Most of the Foresters drew back as she passed by, her face a warning. Those who didn't, died.

Her face had lost the battle glee for which she was so famous. It was cold and intent and unseeing, the cheeks damp with tears and streaked with blood. Robin caught sight of her as she passed and even he dared not approach. There were no barriers to keep her from the door, not even any guards, and she proceeded with deadly intent, through the door and inside the building.

The castle was quieter than the scene outside its wall, but it was littered with wounded Foresters and wailing servants. Torches were the only light and were unstable, flickering and casting lying shadows into every corner. Lily stayed close to the wall, and when it fell away she moved into the space.

It was only a small alcove, three stone walls close together. She ran her hand over the slippery stones, pushing softly, but none moved. Lily repeated the gesture again and noticed a small chip missing from one. The space accepted her finger and she pulled the hidden door open.

Four of the stones had moved to create an opening just large enough to admit a human body. Lily crawled down the long passage, fighting off rats and other vermin, until light appeared ahead, and she slid onto a stone floor.

Death Comes

Why she did not just get up and simply stab him in the back, Lily did not know, but as she crouched against the wall, her sword across her knees, she knew that only one of them would leave this tomb alive.

The sheriff finally turned, a sharp, panicked spin, as though sensing her glare. He drew his sword, his face white as his eyes darted to every corner. The light of the torches made it hard to decipher whether the shadows were just that, or something much more dangerous.

"I'm alone." Lily's smile was chilling and there was death in her eyes. "Don't bother looking for the others."

"You're a foolish girl."

Lily stood up and swung her sword in a wide arc and stopped suddenly, her blade raised, ready to strike. She eyed his bent nose and smiled.

"For a foolish girl I pack a good punch, don't you think?"

He touched his broken nose gingerly and

frowned.

"I hear you're rather good, for a woman," he sneered. Lily glared at him.

"I'm very good, for anyone."

The sheriff didn't answer, only lunged at her. Lily side-stepped the blade. He drew back to strike again before slithering away. His attack was snake-like, but Lily was always ready to block the blows he dealt. She stood her ground and her eyes dared him to attack.

At what point she started to lose the battle, Lily could not tell. Now, she was hard-pressed for space, and the sheriff's blows seemed to come harder and more quickly. Her breath seemed to be catching in her throat as she struggled to gain an advantage.

"You are better than I thought you'd be," he said, as his sword pierced her side in a long, red-hot ribbon of pain and Lily felt her knees buckle. "But you're not the best."

He laughed now, as her hands flew up to stop the steady flow of blood. Her left hand clasped her side, and the blood seeped through her fingers, running down her skin in sticky red rivers. She supported her weight on her right elbow and let her sword lie where it had fallen from her limp fingers.

The room began to fade into a whirlpool of colours and the cold metal poised near Lily's hand bit at her fingers, until she turned and let the blade sink easily into the sheriff's chest. Then, she turned away, no longer caring.

"Guess again," she spit out, in a mixture of blood and hate.

The sheriff gazed in horror and disbelief at the hilt jutting from him. He sank slowly to the floor. Lily curled up on the cold stone and closed her eyes, hardly hearing as the sheriff breathed his death-gasps and was dead.

*****

After they had searched the grounds with ever increasing terror, Will and Robin found her there, lying in her own blood, her eyes closed. They pulled her to her feet, and carried her between them, their shoulders supporting her weight. They helped her outside. Already the sheriff's men were beaten. They streamed past the three of them and into the castle, barring the doors. Robin didn't even turn to look at them. He pushed ahead stubbornly, through the crowd, Lily resting heavily against his shoulder. She made no sound, not even when someone jostled her and he could tell it hurt. She just stared ahead with a vacant look in her eyes.

She didn't look towards the gallows, towards Peter's body. She didn't move or speak when they lifted her onto the wagon, or as Will peeled away the bloody cloth from her skin. Even as he poured alcohol over the wound she didn't whimper. Her eyes were fixed on a point in space which only she could see.

Around them the crowd grew rowdier. The sheriff's death had been discovered, and the celebrations began.

"So, Lily," someone laughed. "We did it! We won this war!"

And finally, Lily spoke. She turned her eyes to him, and the words fell from her mouth with undiluted pain.

"Peter's dead," she said.

She pushed Will away and staggered off, her hand clutching her side. He ran after her, but she shook him off again, her face wet with silent tears.

"I have to go tell Molly." Without another word, she began to run. No one tried to stop her

Molly

Molly moved about the house, her fingers trembling as she laid her grandmother's tablecloth across the rough wood, smoothing it carefully and setting two places on it, pulling up two chairs. She poked the cooking food, sniffing it, stirring it, trying to distract herself. The spoon shook in her hand. She wished she had not sent the children to Aunt Beth's, wished she had them here to hold for a while as she waited.

As the knock sounded on the door she swallowed hard, smoothing her dress, her stomach turning and a pang of fear pierced her heart.

"Please, dear Holy Mother," she whispered. "Bring him home to me today."

She opened the door.

Lily looked up at her, her eyes pools of pure pain, her hands and clothes and face and body covered in blood. The sword at her side was gone, disappeared into someone's body. And Molly knew.

"He's dead?"

Lily nodded. Molly sat down on the step, trying not to cry, swearing to herself that she would be strong before this girl, that she would wait until she was alone, until she could forget the blood that covered this messenger, this benefactor that Molly had never understood.

"Was it quick?"

"He wasn't hanged." Lily paused and a sob ripped from her throat. "He didn't die a criminal. He died honorably, fighting for what he believed. " She shook her head. "Molly, I can't lie. He wasn't fighting. They never gave him a chance to. They shot him."

Molly shook her head. "What do I care if he died fighting or not? If it was honorable or not? He is dead."

She wiped her sweaty hands on her skirt and looked at Lily. "You cry for him and yet you have widowed so many! I am glad he did not die fighting. He hated fighting."

Molly stood up, twisting on her finger the plain wedding band. She looked again at Lily. "You are so young, Lily. Go and be young. Put on a dress and put down your sword. Find love, have babies. Don't ever fight again."

"I have to."

Molly shook her head. "Peter had to. You can escape. Now go. I can't look at you."

Lily looked up at her and Molly could see the complete grief in the girl's eyes, but she had no strength to comfort her. Molly closed the door to the cottage and threw herself on the bed, biting down on the blankets to stifle her sobs, but the sobs were too strong and she screamed them out in the darkness of her home.

Funeral

Will held tightly to Lily's arm, sure she would need his support, but she shook him off, standing straight and proud at the grave, her head held high, knowing that a great many pairs of eyes watched her.

She stood with the mourners, a black cape billowing around her, a black ribbon holding back her hair, but without tears. She had not spoken during the service, not wept or wailed or even sniffled and Will was the only one who seemed to realize her grief. Her eyes betrayed no emotion as the coffin was lowered. She watched Anna and said nothing.

Now the burial was over and the mourners were leaving, but Lily did not move. Will held her arm, pulling gently.

"Let's go."

"Half of these mourners never met him, Will."

"I know."

"How could they possibly miss him? How can they pretend, just because some see him as a hero?

They remember him for the one thing he hated, fighting."

The gravediggers were slowly filling the hole, the shovelfuls of earth thudding as they hit the ground, a calming, rhythmical sound. Lily pulled away from Will and began walking across the grass. She paused as she was passing a large oak tree, under which stood two stones. She froze there, staring at them. Will moved up beside her again.

"What is it?"

"Lily Eleanor Fitzooth," she read, her fingers running over the letters. "Lost Soul. Oh, how well they knew."

She wiped her eyes furiously and spun around, running out of the graveyard and onto Starline. The stallion whirled toward the road, running hard, Lily bent over his neck. Will let her go.

Lily

Will moved through the trees, following the sound of running water and the hoofprints that were indented in the earth. He had followed them from the graveyard but, now that he could hear the river, he moved faster than ever.

The trees fell away and there stood Starline, its muzzle still dripping as it lifted its head from the water. Seeing Will, it returned to drinking. The horse was caked with sweat.

In the river walked Lily, her black funeral cape drenched through, the black ribbon in her hair hanging limply down her dripping back. She stopped walking and sat down, wrapping the cape around herself. The water came up to her chest. Her teeth chattered.

"Lily, what are you doing?" Will stumbled into the river. The water was so cold it sent pain up his legs. Lily didn't move.

"This is where it happened, Will."

"What happened?"

"The drowning." She tucked her knees under her chin. Will stared at the riverbank.

"Here?"

"In water, in a river somewhere. Robin never told me, you know. He never told me how they lost me, but I know." She nodded. "I think I might have always known."

"You remember?"

"No. But I've always hated water." She turned to him. "Remember that day, by the waterfall?"

"When I kissed you," he said. She frowned, then nodded.

"You pulled me into the water and I was so scared. It was painful, that fear. It overwhelms you and envelops you until you can feel nothing but terror." She lifted her hand out of the water and watched in silence as droplets of it formed on her fingertips and fell off. "It doesn't do that anymore. Why couldn't it work today? I needed it today."

Will put his arms around her and tried to lift her, but the cape held her down. "Come on, Lily," he said as he knelt down in front of her. She didn't move as he untied the bow at her neck and let the cape fall off. He glanced at her face. It was white and water ran down it in rivulets. "Your lips are blue."

She shrugged. He pulled her to her feet. She was trembling against him. The hands that clutched his shirt were white and shaking.

"Come on, Lily," he said softly, but she shoved him away.

"No! I don't need to go home! There is no home to go to!"

She walked away from him, her clothes plastered to her, her dark hair falling out of its ribbon and into her face. She trembled and her bad leg shook and almost gave out, but she caught Starline's bridle and did not fall. Instead, she leaned her head against the sweat-laden neck and sobbed, truly cried. For once, all her defenses had broken down. Her body shook and her grip on Starline weakened. She sank to the ground.

The stallion nosed Lily gently in concern as Will moved to her. She didn't fight as he pulled her up into his arms. Instead, she held onto him, burying her face in his shirt to muffle the cries that escaped her.

"It was supposed to be me, Will. I was the one who was supposed to die."

Will nodded and held her, and gently led her to his horse.

Somehow, they made it to the cave. Will pulled the wet garments off her and slipped a white nightgown over her without thinking. She didn't fight, could barely move in her exhaustion. He laid her on the bed and wrapped the blankets around her.

He stumbled into the next room and fell onto

the bed, his every bone and muscle exhausted. His eyes closed and sleep rushed in to envelop him.

In the Morning

When he woke up, Lily lay curled up beside him, her small body taking up little of the bed. Surprised, he sat up on his elbows. The bed creaked under him and she woke up.

"How are you?" he asked.

She shrugged. Her eyes were red and puffy and dried dirt had arranged itself in a thin layer over her skin.

She swung her legs over the side of the bed, stood up, staggered and sat back down again. Will sighed and picked up her pouch. He walked out the door and down the hall, filling it up at the rain barrel before returning to the bedroom.

Lily hadn't moved. Will dipped a handkerchief into the cold water to wipe the dirt from her face.

"So what happened?"

He pulled her to her feet. She shrugged again.

"Why did you go there, Lily?" he asked gently.

"Why not?"

He sighed and continued to wipe her face. Where the dirt had lifted, there was now only clean skin. He wiped around her eyes and saw that she was watching him.

"What is it?"

"You should marry me, Will." She nodded to herself. Will stared at her, then forced a smile.

"So you could have me take care of you all the time?"

She smiled. "That too."

He put the handkerchief away and pulled her to her feet. "Now, go to your room, pick up some clean clothes and trek down to the pool. A bath would do you good."

"A wash, not a bath."

He nodded, remembering the river. "A wash, then."

"Okay," she nodded and turned to leave.

"Lily?" Will's voice stopped her. "You just proposed to me, you know." She nodded.

"I know."

"Did you mean it?"

She smiled. "Will, I wouldn't say it if I didn't mean it."

"I thought that you might have been joking."

She shrugged. "I know." She turned to leave again.

"Lily?"

"What, Will?"

"Yes."

Lily stared at him blankly.

"Yes, I'll marry you."

"Oh." She smiled. "Now can I have my bath?"

"Uh, yes." he stammered, startled. Lily laughed, already herself again, and strode down the hall, disappearing into her room. Will collapsed onto the bed, unable to believe his own happiness.

Two Weeks Later

Lily sat against the tree, the shadows of it even darker than the night's own. She had lost track of time. How long had she sat here this night, in this spot? She had done the same for so many nights now.

She thought suddenly of Marian and felt a twinge of regret that she had not been kinder to Robin's wife. Marian was working so hard on Lily's wedding and yet Lily had skipped three dress fittings. She shook her head. She wasn't sorry anymore.

From the window of the cottage a flickering light peered out into the darkness, creeping under the door, never straying too far. Lily remembered the night Lil was born, how she had sat outside the same cottage with Will, waiting. Peter had been inside the building then, but not now. Inside, she could hear the faint lullaby Peter used to sing to Lil and Anna, sung in Molly's shaky voice now. She sang along softly, burying her mouth and her voice in her neckline.

The singing stopped. Lily could hear Molly talking, but could not hear the words. She was content with the mere sound of the voices of Peter's family.

The cottage door creaked open and Anna stepped outside. She was a dream figure, a waif in a white nightdress with Peter's eyes. Anna ran over the damp grass and stopped at Lily's feet.

"Mama says to come inside."

Lily watched her a little longer until the girl held out her hand. It was Peter's gesture. "Come on."

The cottage was bright and Lily nodded, following dead Peter's child into his home and closing the door behind her.

Love

Will sat in the quiet of the cottage, glancing silently around the simple room. He had planned it and cleaned it and filled it with furniture. There was a fireplace, and a table, and chairs, and shelves, and food, and dishes and in the next room was a bed, covered in a soft blanket. Everything smelt of freshly carved wood and of waiting. After only one more day, he would be married and the rooms would finally be a home.

He bent to stoke the fire and stopped, cold fingers of warning dancing up his spine. Silence reigned, but his thief's ears caught the silence as much as any sound. Why had the night sounds quieted?

Will slipped a knife into his belt and approached the door, his eyes alert. As he stepped outside into the darkness he waited, breathing in the air, his eyes scanning the night.

"Hi." The voice was so familiar, so close.

"Hello, Lily." Then he turned.

She started, then stopped herself, her feet

moving nervously on the ground, her face and hair covered in dirt. Her eyes were white, the colour brilliant in the moonlight. She tried to smile.

"What happened to you?" Will blurted.

She glanced at the dirt-stained clothes and hair and shrugged. "I was in the graveyard. I fell asleep."

"Lily, look at me. You are going to be my wife. You have to talk to me. I can't continue trying to figure out what you really mean. Tell me what is wrong."

"I . . . Oh, God, this is hard." She pulled at her hair. "I . . . I can't . . . I can't marry you."

"What are you talking about?"

Lily shrugged. "I can't do it, Will. I need more. You need more."

"Don't bring what I need into this. I said yes. Remember that? You proposed to me."

"But I don't love you." It was spoken in a low voice, almost a whisper. Will almost crumpled. Lily didn't look at him. "I never loved you. Maybe I thought I did, but I don't. I never will."

"You don't love me?" She shook her head. "Then why did you tell me that you did?"

"Because I knew you loved me!" Her voice was shaky. "I wanted to marry you because I knew that no matter what I do or say or am or what anyone else says, you'll always love me! I was lonely and scared and I needed that." Her voice dropped. "There was no one else."

"Lily, you can't go proposing to people because you've had a hard day! You can't use people like that! I don't know why I bother even telling you this! You've always treated people like this and you always will."

"Will, you'd be miserable with me!" she cried. "I know you. You want a normal family and a normal life, a peaceful existence. I can never live that. I've tried. You deserve this life. I don't."

"Lily, it's over now. We're pardoned. King Richard pardoned us."

She shrugged. "And who pardons him? It's not over. He is still rich and we are still poor and children still die from hunger."

Lily smiled suddenly, a wistful, remembering smile. "Have you ever walked with Robin? Just walked with him through a village, without money or food or anything? I did. The people's faces would just . . . they would come alive! Real honest-to-goodness life would flow through them again! They never saw me. They saw Robin, but I don't want them to see me. I want them to see Robin everywhere, in everybody."

"You can't feed the masses of England by yourself. We've done our part. Rest." Will pleaded with her, but he already knew that she was gone. Lily stared at her hands.

"I was hungry far too often. Children should never be hungry. They forget to be children."

Will tried to look in her eyes, but they were shielded, looking at something that he could not see. He sighed.

"You really mean all this, don't you? You're leaving."

She nodded and tried to smile, but they both knew that the gesture was an empty one. Suddenly, she wrapped her arms around him and held him tightly.

"Thank you," she whispered. "For loving me."

Lily disentangled herself, kissed him on the cheek and turned to the darkness where Starline waited. She leaped up into the saddle.

"You're a good fried, Will Scarlett," she called back to him as she turned the stallion out of the gate and into the night, the leisurely shape of Giant slipping into step behind her. She paused for a moment and glanced over her shoulder. For a moment Will thought that she might turn around, just might come back and he could take her inside the house and they'd never be separated again, but she only smiled and his hopes fell as she raised her arm in a graceful arch and clicked her tongue. Starline moved into a trot and was gone.

Will stood there for a long time, just watching the night sky. It was empty now. He turned to go inside. The cottage seemed empty too. He remembered Lily's laughter and the way she had clung to him in the river, but she was gone. He wondered if it was forever. The risk of that scared him.

"Peter," he whispered. "Did you know how lost she would be without you?"

Sighing, Will rubbed his eyes. There was no one left to answer.

The Author

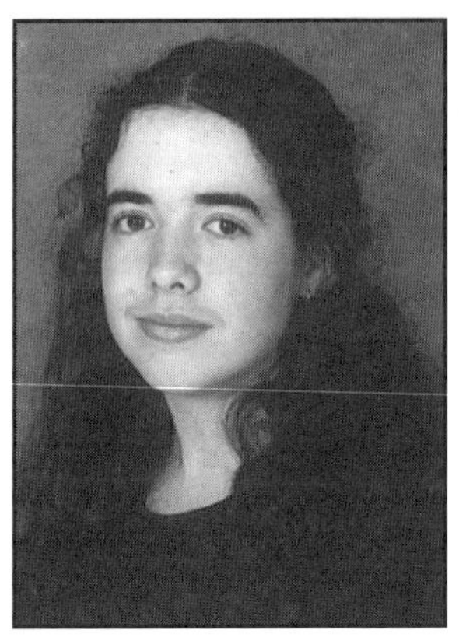

Christina Gunn lives in Whycocomagh, Nova Scotia, with her parents, Anne and Tom Gunn, and her five younger brothers (two older sisters have already left the nest). They all live in L'Arche Cape Breton, a community for mentally handicapped people and the people who choose to share their lives with them.

Christina is a Grade 11 student at Whycocomagh Consolidated School. Besides writing, she plays basketball, rides her horses, baby-sits her little brothers and hangs out with her friends. *Lily* is her first novel.

The Illustrator

Raymond Price was born in Toronto and currently resides in the historic seaside town of Lunenburg, Nova Scotia, with his wife and their three children. He specializes in pen & ink drawings and dry brush watercolour technique.